Brute

Don Jenkins 2018

COPYRIGHT© by Don Jenkins 2018

ISBN-13: 978-1983409745   paperback
ISBN-10: 198340974X

Rev. date: 01/20/2018
Available on AMAZON

Other books by this author: All available on AMAZON

Fallen Petals in the City of Roses   Murder by Proxy
Lucy's Fatal Attraction   The Wayward Drop
Anita and the Iceman   Melanie's Big Bang
The Book Basket (a collection)   Lucky Numbers

Also available on web page full library

Go to: donjenkinsbooks.com

Contents

Brute
Chapter 1   Love is Where You Find It

Robert was seated at one of those small round tables with three chairs, in Logan's Bar on the corner of 10th Street and E. Hedding Street. This is an area just NW of the Luna Park District on the west side of San Jose. It was one of his favorite water holes. It was Friday night with the weekend stretching ahead. A perfect time to relax and forget the weekly turmoil.

Robert was on his second drink of scotch and soda when she walked in. It was only on rare occasions, that he got lucky enough to hook up in the bar. It was not really his quest. But one never knows, when something special might happen. Speaking of special, this one was all of that. She had a brazen aura about her, and was proudly displaying her attributes. Mainly, no bra and cleavage that left little to the imagination. The face above the cleavage was stunningly beautiful. Auburn hair, green eyes, and cheeks just rosy enough not to be overdone. There seemed to be a cloud of adventure with a hint of danger about her.

There was enough suggestiveness to attract the attention of three men at the end of the bar closest to the front door. The smoothest of the three, took a step back from the bar and encountered the lady as she walked in. "Hey there nice lady, allow me the honor of being the first to buy you a drink tonight."

"Sorry sir. I am here to meet my fiancé. And there he is, at the table over there." With this rebuff she sauntered over to Robert's table and stood next to his chair. She bent over and kissed him on the cheek. She whispered close to his ear," please play along. That guy gives me the creeps. I couldn't think fast enough to tell him to go fuck himself."

"I am glad to play your decoy. No problem. Would you care to have a seat? That is until the creep is out of the picture."

She sat down next to him and whispered "thanks".

"Without falling into the creep category, may I buy you a drink?"

"I could use one as long as there are no strings attached."

"No strings. You've got it." He waved to the barmaid with two fingers. She came over to his table. He ordered another scotch and soda, and asked his new maybe friend, what she would like. The answer was margarita with crushed ice.

"I guess it's time for introductions", she halfway smiled. "My name is Alexis Struthers. I'm from Eugene, Oregon. I'm here for a seminar with the beauty products company, I work for. Tomorrow is the last session, and then I'm off to Oregon."

"My name is Robert Jonathon Barclay. My friends call me Rob. I'm here on a mission of life. I live just a couple of miles from where we sit. A die hard local."

"Well Robert. May I call you Rob?"

"Only if you can pass the sentry test."

"And, that is?"

"Halt. Who goes there, friend or foe?"

"Friend."

"Okay. You can call me Rob."

"Well Rob, please call me Alee since we are now bonafide friends. I am just a bit off course just now.

(2)

Every man, that I have come close to today has hit on me. I guess I should be flattered, but it becomes a little annoying after about the fifth hit." She said this with a little girlish look on that beautiful face. A somewhat bemused look. Like, I really don't know what the fuss is all about. "First it was the waiter at the conference. Then the invited speaker. Believe it or not, even the cabbie on the way from the hotel to here. And you saw what I encountered here."

"Alee, I would think you might want to take inventory. Then you might figure it out. First, do you ever wear a bra?"

"Shit. You men sure stick together. It's my fault, because of the way, I try to look attractive, and comfortable."

"All I am saying is, that you are one beautiful woman with sexiness oozing all over the place. And, I'm willing to bet a month's salary, that those babies are the real McCoy."

"That's one bet, you win hands down. Give me your hand." She reached over with her right hand, and took his left hand in hers. She pulled Rob's hand up to her right breast and planted it dead on. "Now does anything feel phony about that?" She was so dead-panned, that Rob was amused. Her expression was that of a woman asking the city bus driver, if he stopped at Mission Street and 24th.

"All I can say is, I'm sorry I didn't get that bet down in time. No, there isn't any sign of tampering with the goods."

Alexis gave a small giggle. "I think I like you. You are straight to the point. You don't hold back. You would

(3)

probably have me in tears, if I stay around too long. And what makes you think you could have found a taker on that bet?"

"Think nothing of it. I was only fighting fire with fire. I don't see you as someone who's going to go all teary. I see you as a person, that will not take too much bull. You can take it, and you can dish it out. I've already made up my mind about you. The results are in. You win the election for who's the prettiest and most intelligent woman I've met this month. Maybe year. As for a taker. I would have given odds. There's always a sap who can't resist odds."

"Rob, you are too much. I mean that in a good way. I bet you keep the locals breathing hot and heavy."

The two newly bonded friends sat, and had another round of drinks. She told him a few things about Eugene and how much she loved that town. She wasn't married, and when she asked him if he was, the reply was, "Not today, yesterday, nor anytime soon." Alexis was studying the guy, computing his charms. Were they superficial or well rooted? Was he just another asshole, who was looking for a quick hump in the hay, or was there some depth to his easy-going nature. His eyes didn't give anything away. They seemed sincere. But there was also a hint of mischievous promise of bad boy behavior. She liked those eyes. They were a deep blue. They had the power of deep penetration. She knew, that she would have to be careful of her thoughts. Those penetrating eyes would pierce through and read her soul. She began to feel a girlish nervousness. She recognized the symptoms. She was falling prey to his aura. Hormones were sending signals. Promise of adventure was beckoning to her. 'What have I got to lose?'

(4)

"Say Rob, are you one of those kind that believes in kissing on first date?" This said with a demurring smirk.

"Hell babe. I haven't got my mind around this being a first date. It's more like a first encounter."

"Then, let me rephrase the question. Do you believe in kissing on first encounter?"

"If the answer to that question was no, that would be a rule about to be sorely tested." This he said with a toying lecherous smile.

"Then, I guess the only remaining question is, your place or mine?"

The answer to that last question was, to continue their conversations at Rob's house, which was not far away. She had arrived at the bar in a taxi, so she would simply ride along with him in his car.

The house was in an upscale neighborhood. Rob's pad was as good from the front as any in the area. It was a single level four-bedroom affair. However, it only hosted one bedroom. Rob had converted three bedrooms in the very back, into a work-lab. He had closed off two of the doors, and entry was made into the lab through a single entry. It had the same lock style as the front door with the thumb print reader.

At the front door Alexis spouted, "Now that is something new. I have heard of fingerprint reading locks before. But this has got to be the first time, I have seen one on a front door of a house."

"It's a new item my company worked up. Its computer controlled from the inside. You simply lift up this lid, and the plastic card face with the small circle, is where I place my thumb. The stored image in the computer recognizes the authenticity of the print image. When you hear the buzz and click, you know you're in. The small red light there at the bottom turns green at the same time the lock is opened.

It isn't on the open market yet. We are running tests on it at several locations. Mine being one."

The two had barely entered the front door into the living room, when Alexis threw her arms around Robert as she feverishly searched for his mouth with hers. Contact was quickly achieved and the ensuing kiss was long and full of savoring urgency.

"Alee, you take my breath away. And I do mean that literally."

He led her into the one functioning bedroom. They began tearing at one another's clothes. The chore of removing garments was hindered by the refusal, of either to give up on the savage pursuits of their lips.

The standard size bed became their refuge. It became the platform for that most intimate of human bonding. Lust is the impetus with one goal in store; that of sensual release of stored up passion. The longer in storage the greater the urgency for release. For Alexis, it had been in storage for over two months. For Robert, it had been six weeks. For young people in their early thirties, anything over two days can be demanding.

It had been a writhing symphony of bodies' in motion. It had built fast and furiously up to the crescendo, of two mind shattering, gasping eruptions. It was as if, the air in the room had become a cocoon, embroiling the two lovers in an aura of mysticism. There was no world outside of the cocoon. They might as well, have been on some far distant planet.

(6)

Once the accomplished feat of desire had been met, comes the afterglow with its own human satisfactions. Yet wrapped together, there was the solid body comfort of two melded into
one. The firm yet softness of two bodies held close together. A moment one would hold onto in earnest fear of dissipation.

Saturday morning, the two lovers were up and about. Alee was busy in the kitchen making breakfast. She was in a gay mood. She had made love to Rob twice last night and once before getting out of bed this morning. She felt completely rejuvenated. She had been the queen of the ball. Hopefully her carriage would not turn into a pumpkin. What the hell, midnight had already passed and nothing had changed. That is, not to the bad. Everything was wine and roses. A new kind of joy and happiness was afoot. What were the odds. A quick stop at a bar and there he was. Mr. wonderful. Mr. Oh' so right. Now she could only hope to keep the relationship afloat. It's too soon to say anything about Wade. That could wait. Wait until the right time.

After the savory breakfast, Rob popped the question," What time is your session this morning?"

"Starting time is nine. It should take fifteen minutes to get there. So, we've got half an hour until I blast out of here. Should I call a taxi, or you up to giving me a lift?"

"I can do that. But what about after? I mean, do you have to leave today? I would love it, if you could see your way, to laying over another day. Tomorrow is Sunday. Surely, you don't have any commitments on Sunday. It would give us a chance to become better acquainted."

"Rob Dear, you have twisted my arm. I would love to stay one more day. I'm glad you asked. I was about to

(7)

suggest the same thing. But, I was afraid to take the lead. I mean you are the host, no? I am a little bit afraid, I may have made a bad impression last night. I may have given you the wrong idea
about me. You know, an easy pickup in a bar. That might put the slut brand on me. I mean, what were you to think?"

"I would never think that. Besides if I did, what would that make of me. Or, are we to use the old double standard. You a slut, me a stud. Let's not even go there. I like to think, we met by pure circumstance. The magnetism was there, and it brought us where we now stand." They were standing by the kitchen sink. He took her in his arms and held her close. He stroked her Auburn hair and kissed her gently on the mouth. "I'm all for getting to know each other better. I do mean much better. I don't want you to go away, with the notion, that I cruise bars, for a quick hump in the hay. Please do stay as long as you possibly can."

"Well put. I think we have cleared that little item up quite succinctly. Don't ask me why, but I never thought of you cruising the bars for chicks. I guess, that makes me feel somewhat special. Thank god for that old voodoo magnetism. Now we have work to do. I've got to change my flight home. I need to check out of the Holiday Inn. Will you go with me, or do I go solo?"

"Are you kidding? I don't intend to let you out of my sight. Let's hit the pavement."

She asked, "What about the 9:00 O'clock company seminar session?"

"No problem. I'll sit quietly in the corner and be a good boy."

"Well, maybe we can cut it short and scoot out early."

(8)

Alexis stayed with Robert Saturday. She cut short her last session. Saturday was spent without interruption by any family
or friends. Robert did have one telephone call from his older brother Steve. Other than that, the two newly bonded lovers were undisturbed as they got to know each other better. Alexis was fascinated by Rob's work with Digital Autonomous Intelligent Programs or 'DAIP'. Rob did not equate the company's products with artificial intelligence. Their creations were not thinking machines. They were rather integrated with algorithms and digital command positions. They did not learn on their own, or have the ability for independent thinking. However, they were top-notch at solving a variety of input data, that required processing and sorting. In effect, they did have equipment, that appeared to be actually thinking. Rob's brother was the CEO of the firm. He had started with them when they were in the start -up stage. He owned a large bundle of stock in the corporation, and sat on the board of directors as well as being the CEO. He had recruited his younger brother straight out of college. That was seven years ago. Robert came into the firm with a master's degree in computer science. His brother had gone the whole nine yards and had attained a PhD in the same field. The only problem, was that Robert did not share his brother's commitment to the firm. He somewhat enjoyed the work of writing apps and working design concepts. He didn't care much for all the hoopla over future goals and marketing. He was strictly a nine to five. Once out of the office, her pursued his own ambitions. He had built his own work-lab in the back bedrooms of his house. He loved to tinker with his own ideas. He had tens of thousands of dollars invested in his little man cave. It was more than

merely a hobby. It was a way of exercising creativity.

Alexis on the other hand, lived a quainter life in terms of career choice. She sold beauty products for 'Lady Carmen'. She was in effect an independent agent. It was all based on commissions. She had established her market in Eugene, and was doing very nicely. She hadn't won a pink Cadillac yet, but perhaps someday. She loved Eugene. She was born there and had no desire to ever relocate. She told Rob about her various friends, some comical anecdotes, and some that were more drama oriented. She had decided the time wasn't quite right yet, to mention Wade.

Sunday morning, Robert took her to the San Jose airport. Her plane lifted of at eleven. They had had a terrific and prolific round of love making Saturday afternoon and that night. Sunday morning would be the last round of this match. They had seemed so perfectly suited to one another, that Rob suggested he should make the journey to Eugene. Just to see how beautiful the town really was. She had given it a powerful build-up. Naturally, he was more interested in seeing her again than he was about the town. The plan was made for Rob to make the trip in two weeks. He would put in for earned vacation time. No problem.

After seeing Alexis off at the airport, Robert drove to his brother's house and rang the doorbell. Patricia, Steve's wife, answered the chimes. "Hello Bobby. Good to see you. Come on in. Steve is in the den."

Robert hated to be called Bobby. It made him feel like a juvenile. But he dearly loved Pat, so he let it slide. Anybody else, he would have given them a tutorial on proper name calling.

(10)

He gave her a 'you're a part of the family hug', and teasingly said," What makes you think I give a damn about Steve. Maybe I came to see you. You, luscious doll."

"You are quite the flirt. Someday, I'm gonna shock you out of your socks, and flirt right back." Her grin was, that of the politician being handed a new bribe.

"Well, just be careful. You know how much I love you." With the repertoire running its course, they both chuckled and Rob went on towards the den to visit with big brother.

"Hello, hello. Dr. Einstein, I presume." Steve's little jibe.

"At your service Doc. Looks like I caught you reading. What is it, a computer magazine, the company's monthly report, or a sleazy crime and sex novel?"

"Little brother, what brings you to the lion's den. Don't tell me you have a new invention you want to sell me."

"Not this time. I wanted to let you know, I met someone this weekend. A lady as it were. A real special lady. She hails from Eugene, Oregon. I mean to tell you Stevio, this one is super special. I think, I'm head over heels for this one. We just spent the last two days together. I dropped her at the airport an hour ago. I plan to take my two weeks and go up there to visit."

"Rob, don't you think you may be rushing things a bit. Don't tell me you believe in love at first sight. I know you better than that. Maybe, lust at first sight. You've been flying solo too long. What's it been since Marge? Two months? Man, you're still healing over that one. Let's say, you just met someone, who turned out to be a good dose of medicine for what ails you."

(11)

"Shit Steve, if its medicine we're talking about, then let's face it. I've become addicted to it. And you can bet your ass, I'm cured as far as Marge is concerned."

"What the hell. I can see, you are going to rush into this thing. I guess, it will play out one way or another. As far as vacation time, you have it coming. It's your call how you spend it. I wish you the best of luck on this one. It's about time for you to settle down."

Rob had lunch with Steve and Pat before heading back to his home. He was glad that Steve understood his plight. Steve had great influence on him. He was always there in times of need or consultation. It was Steve, that pushed him to finish college, and the two years of post-graduate for his Masters. It was also he, that got him his position at DAIP. The big brother relationship had been there from the start. During childhood it was Steve that interceded when older boys bullied Rob. All through life to present, Steve was there to defend him from societal ills. Rob couldn't imagine life and all the bullshit, without Steve there as a buffer.

Chapter 2 The Visit North

Robert caught the early flight on Alaska Air and arrived in Eugene at eight, Saturday morning late July. She was there to greet him at the gate. As lovely as he remembered her from two weeks ago. Sometimes it takes a second encounter to balance a first impression. There could have been flaws overlooked. But not this time around. If anything, she was more beautiful than his recollection of the first meeting. They gathered up his luggage and were off to her residence. It was a one level three-bedroom affair in the Coburg Road area. A nice quite neighborhood with well-groomed yards and plenty of foliage. Several with roses and bushy Rhododendrons. He could see the salutary effect the area received from so much rain fall. It was as if, a city was carved out of a luscious forest. There was the majestic Willamette River flowing right through the center of it all. He began to understand, her affinity for her town.

The two lovers were at Alexis' house and wasted no time in renewing their bonding. Mornings are a good time to start the day off with passionate cuddling. Love making after two weeks of separation had a special caveat. It is said, that 'separation makes the heart grow fonder'. These two hearts were made just that. After making love, the two made plans for the weekend, which was already well started. It was late July, therefore a trip to the Oregon Coast was in order. Except for the rush of tourists at the coast, it was indeed a grand time to be there. They would walk the beaches. Stay overnight in a motel with beach frontage. Taste the variety of available local seafood at the many local restaurants. The city was Newport. The very core of the coastal tourist attraction. People came from

California, Washington, Idaho, and just about any state in the country. The waters off the shore are not as warm as other coastal

attractions such as Southern California, but the beauty of the scenic shores and beaches are something to behold.

Saturday night Rob and Alee sat on the beach at an open beach fire. A simply built fire utilizing a beached log. A common type of doing on the Oregon Coast. All you need is a high and dry log, and a little bit of kindling, and you have a fire that will burn long into the starry night. With the bottle of Pinot Greis and two wine glasses, the evening was set for romance and easy relaxation. Other couples surrounded the fire and conversations abounded. This was a new type of outing for Rob. Alexis made the affair complete. He felt very complete. More complete than ever before in his life.

The weekend at the beach was forever etched in Rob's memory. It was one of the happiest weekends, he could ever remember. The following week in Eugene went seemingly too fast. They hiked the local buttes, jogged the bike trails, and spent lazy days picnicking at Fern Ridge Lake. The lake was cool, but refreshing. Rob and Alee swam in the area close to the docks. The setting couldn't be any better except for the hazy smoke-filled sky. It was a bad year for Oregon all over. There were seven forest fires blazing around various parts of the state. Some were close enough to Eugene to fill the sky with onerous smoke. The news was, that the Feds refused to allow the state to respond to a fire that was small and manageable at just a few acres. The governor of Oregon had requested permission to put out the fire which was on Federal lands, while in its initial stages. The Federal Government Land

(14)

Management Department refused the request. In the end game, the fire destroyed 400,000 acres of timberland. The Feds always know best. The Willamette valley would suffer throughout the summer with smoke filled sky's, and no rain in sight to put an
end to the horrendous fires. What would otherwise have been a perfect summer; the smoke took its toll. Outdoor activities were stymied by the foulness in the air.

The following Saturday morning there was a break in the smokey atmosphere. It had to do with winds, coming and going in the right direction, so as to spare the Eugene Metro area. Rob had awoken at seven in the morning. He nudged his sleeping partner and when she fluttered her eyes, he asked if she wanted to take a jog with him. She reached out and took his hand and said, "Not this morning. I need more sleep." She reached up and touched the bandage on his right cheek. "Rob, I'm so sorry about that. I don't know what got into me."

Rob tried to reassure her it was nothing. She had suffered a bad dream, and struck out her arm. Her hand came across his check with two dragging fingernails. He awoke with a yelp. She was flailing about. He grabbed her shoulders and shook her gently. Her eyes opened with the look of terror stamped on her face.

"Baby. You were having a bad dream. It must have been a whopper. You were fighting for dear life."

"It must have been that damn Wade." She had told Rob about her relationship with Wade Brendon. The impetus for bringing it out in the open, had occurred two days ago. Wade had showed up at Alee's house, with the pretense of returning a music CD. She had opened the front door and there he stood. In direct violation of the

(15)

restraining order, she had placed on him. He even had the gall to ask if he could come in and talk. She replied that if he did not go away and now, she would call the police. Wade then noticed Rob in the background. A quick expression of furry crossed his face. Neck muscles were strained. "I see you didn't waste any time in finding another dick to suck."

She slammed the door shut. She looked through the peephole. He stood there looking furious for a moment. She yelled through the door. "Wade, I'm calling the police."

"Fuck you bitch." With this last outburst, he turned and begin to walk down the street.

Rob was bewildered. "Whoa, sweetheart. What the hell was that all about?"

"That was Wade. I was about to tell you about him. We went together for a couple of years. I had a bad time with him towards the end. He was insanely jealous. Any man I talked to on the phone, or on the street, became fodder for vicious attacks. At first, they were only verbal. Then one afternoon, I had just got off the phone with a friend, and he started in. This time it got real ugly. He began hitting me. At first, with open-handed slaps. Then he began punching me. I ended up in emergency. I immediately filed charges, and obtained a restraining order. He spent thirty days in jail. Today is the first encounter since then. Then was over two months ago. The crazy thing is, I never cheated on him. I meant to tell you all bout it sooner. Please don't be angry with me for waiting so long. I had no idea there would be any more trouble from him."

"No problem. Now it's in the open. If the creep shows up again, my advice is, do not talk to him. Call the police immediately." Rob was concerned that the man obviously had a violent side. He was not otherwise put off about the revelation of the relationship. She was a grown beautiful woman. He would have had to been insane, had he not allowed for the fact, there was most likely someone before he came along.

So, this Saturday morning he would take his jog solo. Let Alee get her beauty sleep. It had been a rough night for her. He hoped the nightmares would not be often re-occurring. In that event, he then, would need to wear a catcher's face mask to bed.

He left her to her cozy nest, and headed out the door with his spandex running pants and Nike track shoes, and band aide on his cheek. He planned to go for four or five miles.

Chapter 3   Sudden Awakening

Wade sat in his car, half a block from Alee's house. He had been there since six, this Saturday morning. It was now seven thirty. The front door to Alee's opened, and out came the dude he had seen in the house earlier in the week. She was undoubtedly shacking up with him. She was the slut he had always suspected her of being. The dude was geared for sports. He took off jogging down the street. This would be a good time to call on the bitch, and maybe teach her a lesson.

Once the jogger was out of sight, Wade exited his car and walked the half block to the house. He avoided the front door. He knew if he rang the doorbell, Alee would most likely peep through the small hole, and upon seeing him, call the police. He took the circuitous route around the back yard. He hoped to find an open window. He checked each outside window until he found one that was ajar. It was a spare bedroom window that was slightly open. He pulled off the outside screen and gently pushed the window to the right until it was wide open. Being stealthily quiet, he hoisted himself up upon the window sill, and pulled his body into the room. Once on his feet in the spare bedroom, he slowly, and without fanfare, crossed the room and opened the door. He walked down the hall and checked the kitchen and living room. She was not in sight. Wade walked back down the hall and slowly opened the master bedroom door. He could see she was still in bed. 'Probably been fucking all night.' He sidled up to the side of the bed. She was laying on her right side on the left portion of the bed. He sat on that side of the bed.

He reached down and shook her by the shoulders. She began to stir. She rolled over to her left a bit, propped herself up and looked towards the figure on the bed beside her.

"Hello bitch. I just want you to know you've been fucking with the wrong guy." The words had barely left his lips, when he slapped her a few hard licks.

Her only utterance was, "Wade, no, my god no." It was not a scream. More akin to a desperate moan. It would be the last to come out of her mouth. No sooner were the words expelled, there came a hard-fisted blow to her jaw. It came with the sickening sound effects of flesh and bone being torn and broken. The blow came so furiously, that she was propelled on over to her back. She now lay staring at the ceiling. Wade immediately jumped up on her still body, and with both knees crushing against her thighs, he reached down with both hands and grasped her throat tightly. He applied all the pressure he could muster. Her legs began to writhe and kick, fighting against the force that was subjugating her. All this, even though she was unconscious. Very soon the movements came to a sudden and meaningful stop. Meaning that there was nothing left to resist. Nothing left to fight with.

Wade knew the exact moment that she had expired. He knew it with a certainty. He backed off from the abused throat. He looked down at her. He felt a great triumph. He had taught the cheating bitch, she couldn't get away with her ball busting ways. Now, all that was left, was to commemorate the moment. He was set to do just that. He pulled out of his pocket a small Sony camera. The kind that's not much bigger than a business card. It operates by pulling down the small chrome bar that covers the lens.

(19)

This would automatically turn on the power, and the camera was ready to shoot.

He propped his trophy up on two pillows, putting her in a slightly elevated position from waist up. He snapped a good shot, with the breasts visible in the frame. He thought. 'she doesn't look like such hot shit now.'

"What do you think Alee? Do you feel like hot stuff now? You won't be fucking over anybody else. I did your boyfriend a favor." He felt a slight shiver. He knew she was dead, but it was, as if she could still communicate with him. It gave him the creeps. It was time to make his exit. He had his trophy picture tucked away in his camera. It figured to be a lasting memento of his triumph over the witch. The entire event had a sexual overtone to it. It gave him a stupendous feeling of power, that caused arousal. He would have a surprise for Karen this morning.

He left the residence as he had entered. Back out through the window, and replacement of the bug screen. He checked the ground where he had entered and exited. He found no disturbance on the hard ground. He walked slowly around the house and once more through the side gate. Once inside his car, he surveilled the street from end to end. There was no one in sight. He slowly drove away from the curb and down the street. Everything had gone better than planned. He drove towards Karen's house, where he had been staying for the last month. She was something of an airhead, but she treated him with great affection. The sex was not bad, but nothing like Alexis. The main thing was, she didn't give him any shit. His word was the final authority in all their interplays. She was very subservient to him. Early in the relationship, he had found an excuse to knock her around a bit. It was mostly

(20)

intended to show her the score. To let her know who was boss, and that he would not tolerate any disobedience. Today, he would have her scripted to say, that he had not left the house this morning. He knew he could count on her obedience.

Chapter 4   The Primary Crime Scene

Robert finished his five miles and panted up to the front door. He pulled the key out of the small pouch on his waist band and unlocked the door. Alee was nowhere in sight. He moseyed down to the main bedroom and peeked in. She was sitting up with her eyes wide open. It didn't look natural. Not natural at all. He stepped into the bedroom. She didn't blink. The unnaturalness now became bizarre. He felt a cold shiver run up his back. He hastened to the bedside and muttered her name. Still no response. He touched her wrist and felt for a pulse. He did not expect to feel one. He did not. He noticed a slight puffiness under her right eye. She looked cold. There was no sign of a living human. She was gone.

Robert then, burst into tears. He sat on the edge of the bed in the same spot her violator had sat just an hour earlier. He touched her hand and moaned her name. He then, pulled himself together and called 911. He reported the discovery of his friend, obviously murdered. He gave the address and his name. The woman on the other end, told him to stay with the deceased, and a crew would be there momentarily.

Within five minutes the first police squad car pulled up. One of two officers rang the doorbell. Robert answered and asked them in. One of the officers had his note book out, and was ready to take notes. While answering questions, Robert walked the officers to the scene. One officer walked up close to the bed and felt Alee's wrist for a pulse. He stepped back and declared she was apparently dead. He was very cautious about disturbing the body. "It's best if we all step out of the room. We do not want to disturb any possible evidence."

The three men stepped out into the hallway. More questions were asked, as one of the officers called into headquarters. He gave a terse report on the discovery. He requested a medical examiner right away. He asked to relay his report to Sgt. Garcia.

Within fifteen minutes the house was a buzz with several officers including Sgt. Garcia. It was the Sgt.'s job to secure the crime scene. Being the first location to enter the journal of criminal activity, this would be classified as the 'Primary Crime Scene.' The Sgt. Ordered his men to tape off the bedroom and the entire surrounding of the house. He had a man take pictures of the entire scene inside of the house and outside as well.

Detective Brad Ferguson and his aide Detective Matt Wagner came into the scene. Jennifer Caldwell, the deputy Medical Examiner was there with her crew. In all death situations, it was the medical examiner's office, that took full responsibility for the body. They were the only ones to study the body close up. It was their duty to estimate the time of death and cause, when it was evident. In criminal deaths, a full autopsy was required by the medical examiner. The autopsy when completed, would be the final word on exact time of death as well as the cause.

Brad and Matt scoured the house for any evidentiary clues. They queried Robert.

Brad; "What was your relationship with the lady?"

Robert; "I was in love with her. We just met a couple of weeks ago in San Jose, where I live. It was a quick get to know one another. We clicked right off. She was so terrific and beautiful. We spent the weekend together, and I promised to come up and visit her here."

(23)

Brad; "How did you come by the wound on your cheek? Do you mind pulling off the band aide?"

Robert didn't hesitate. He reached up and gently pulled away the rather large band aide. In doing so, he exposed two scratch marks on his cheek.

Brad; "Can you explain those scratches? They look rather recent."

Robert was about ready to explain the scratches when a red flag went up inside his head. "Tell me officer. Am I to be considered a suspect? Are you even thinking about arresting me?"

"Why do you ask? Is there a possible reason we should consider you a suspect?"

"I have never been arrested in my life. But I have heard of people, incriminating themselves unwittingly. I definitely do not want to misspeak and create any intimation of guilt."

"In other words, you are feeling cautious. It is not our intention to incriminate you by any trick questions. You have to realize, that you are, as of now, a person of interest. Simply by the fact, you were possibly the last person to see the victim alive other than her killer. The fact you were in a relationship with her puts you on the list of persons of interest. Before this is solved, there most likely will be several people on that list. It becomes a matter of elimination. The actual killer may come from out of the blue. That is to say, persons of interest may never rise to the threshold of suspects. It's just a normal police procedure to get all the information from people having contact with the victim. You are free to call an attorney before you answer any further questions. In the very near future, we may be forced to bring you in for more questions. You should not make any plans to leave this jurisdiction until that time."

Robert; "I'll take a chance. I certainly have nothing to hide. Ask away."

Brad had a sudden feeling that the man was on the level. "Okay, fair enough. If any question I pose bothers you, you can defer until you have an attorney to advise. Remember, no tricks on our part. All I am looking for are honest explanations. Let's start with the cheek marks."

"It happened early this morning. I was asleep. About three AM. Alee starts moaning and writhing about. She was flinging her arms. One hand caught me on the cheek. I was not even awake at that moment. Well, I sure woke up in a hurry when I felt the sting on my face. I turned toward her and shook her gently. It was a very traumatic moment. She woke up and admitted she had been having a terrible dream. I soothed her down. I got up and washed my face and put that big band aide on the scratches."

"Anything else happen the rest of the night?"

"No. She finally went back to sleep. Soon after, I drifted off as well."

"So, morning rolled around and you got up and left her in bed?"

"Yes. But first, I woke her up, and asked if she wanted to go jogging with me. She said no. She was still sleepy. We had kept each other up quite late last night. I told her I would probably
be gone for an hour. I wanted to get in four or five miles."

"So, you did your run, and came back and let yourself in. You went into the bedroom land found her dead on the bed. Did you touch the body?"

(25)

"I felt her wrist for a pulse. I was pretty sure she was gone."

"Then you called 911. How long did you wait to make the emergency call?"

"Just a couple of minutes. I needed to get myself together first. I was shattered by finding her like that. I mean, just an hour or so earlier, she was alive and in good humor. I loved her very much. I intended to marry her. I hadn't popped the question yet. Now it will never be." He began to moist around the eyes. He felt a slight tremble in his body.

Brad noticed the sudden emotional signals. "Take it easy. I know how it must hurt. I won't ask any more questions for now. Do me a favor, and come down to the station Monday morning. If you like, bring an attorney. For now, I do need a DNA swab sample. Are you willing to volunteer one? I'll also need to take a photo of the facial scratches."

Rob complied and did a mouth swab for the detective.

Brad took a few photos of his face, and a long shot showing his full frame and attire. Rob retired to a guest bedroom and stretched out on the queen-sized bed. He held the pillow close to his face and sobbed. The police were still swarming in the rest of the house and yard.

Deputy Medical Examiner, Jennie Caldwell, had been working over the corpse. She was finishing up, and held a small plastic baggie in her hand. "Brad, you may be interested in this. I have skin particles taken from the victim's fingernails. It appears she may have put up a fight."

"Well, yes and no. Her boyfriend tells me, she awoke from a bad dream, kicking and swinging. She caught him

(26)

across the cheek as he was asleep. He's bearing the marks. What I will be interested in, is the time and cause of death."

"For preliminary purpose, I put the death at around seven thirty this morning. We will be able to be more definite after the autopsy. I am ninety percent sure the victim was choked to death. She died from asphyxiation. Again, wait for the autopsy for real sure. She was hit in the face pretty hard also. There is only slight abrasion due to the fact, she died before swelling and bruising could occur. However, there is enough there to show the effect of a hard blow. It looks as if the jaw may have been fractured. You should have our full autopsy report in a couple of days. Unless you object, I'll send the skin particles up to Multnomah for DNA testing. Perhaps you can get us a match test sample."

Brad dangled the kit bag he had tested on Robert. "You can test with this. I am pretty sure it will be a match"

In the spare bedroom, Rob suddenly pulled himself away from his refuge and bolted onto the floor. He suddenly realized he was not the only one to suffer this tragic loss. Her mom and dad would be devastated when told. He hustled back down the hall to where Brad and his partner were poking around.

"Detective. What about her mother and father? Who's to tell them?"

"That's up to us. Do you have information on them?"

"I only met them once. Alee took me to meet them. They live off 30th Avenue up in the south hills. I don't recall the address. I know, Alee has their phone number in her contacts on her cell-phone under dad."

"I would ask, that you let us contact them in person. It's better that way. Please do not call them until we have

(27)

the opportunity to visit them. We should be up there within the next hour. Seeing as how, you have come to some grips, is there anything else you can tell us at this point?"

"You may want to check out her ex-boyfriend, Wade Brendon. You should have a file on him. She had a restraining order on him. He came to the front door a couple of days ago on the pretense of returning a music CD. She became angry, and ordered him to leave, with the threat of calling the police. I asked her what it was all about. She had not previously mentioned the guy. She told me, that she went out with him for a couple of years. They had broken up over two months ago. She said, in her own words, 'it had gotten ugly at the end'. He had beaten her badly. She ended up in emergency. That's when she filed charges, and sought the restraining order. He spent thirty days in jail. She was definitely afraid of him."

"Well, that certainly makes him a person of interest. We will check him out. Thanks for the heads up. We would have eventually come across the information, but this will speed it up some. I'll need to ask you to take up quarters somewhere other than here. The house will be a crime scene that will need to not be disturbed. Will that be a problem for you?"

"No. I am sure I can find a motel. I wouldn't want to stay here now."

Chapter 5   Inquiries

Brad and Matt drove up the south hills to the Struthers' residence. They approached the front door and rang the doorbell. Mr. Edward Struthers answered. He appeared to be in his late sixties, with slightly graying hair and short beard. He was dressed casually, but yet stylish. He smelled of lingering cigar smoke. He asked the gentleman what he could do for them. Very mannerly.

Brad; "I am Detective Brad Ferguson. This is my partner Detective Matt Wagner. I am afraid we have terrible news to have to bring you."

"Somebody died?" He asked with deadly foreboding. His mind was racing. Like a computer, scrambling the possibilities of what could possibly follow such an ominous opening salvo.

"Can we come in. It is a great tragedy I have to relay. I think it would be better if we were inside."

"Come in." The possibilities running through Edward's mind were becoming focused on close family. "Has something happened to Alexis?"

Inside the living room, Brad stood close to Edward, and told him his daughter had been murdered in her bed. The reaction from the father was strange. He did not go weak at the knees. His expression was placid, not showing any registry of grief inside. "Can you tell me the facts of the case? Was she shot, stabbed, or beaten with a blunt object?" It might have been questions being put forth by an investigator.

"We have at this time, reason to believe, that she was strangled." Brad searched the man's eyes. There was no formation of tears. He was totally stoic.

(29)

"I suppose you will want me to come and identify the body. I will have to break the news to Myrna, my wife. It will be a terrible blow I'm afraid. Do you have any idea, who might have killed my daughter?"

"At this point, we only have a couple of people of interest. What do you know about a young man from California? His name is Robert Barclay."

"I only know, that Alexis was crazy about him. I met him once here at the house. Alexis brought him here to meet my wife and me. He seemed like a very nice man. Very polite and seemingly intelligent. I certainly hope he is not on your list of possibles."

"It's too soon to tell. He is co-operating with us. You are aware that he was staying with your daughter?"

Then it happened. The old man let out an uncontrolled moan and sank to his knees. It happened so fast, that neither Brad nor Matt had time to put hands on him, before he toppled to the floor. He was out cold. The most sudden fainting spell Brad had ever witnessed. He had seemed so in control right up to that moment. To make matters darker, Myrna came into the room at the instant Edward hit the floor. She gasped, "oh my god."

Brad and Matt together, grabbed Edward under the shoulder and walked him over to the sofa. Brad turned to Myrna and could see the fear in her eyes. "Mrs. Struthers, I'm from Eugene Police. My name is Detective Ferguson. This is Detective Wagner. I'm afraid we are here on sad business." As he began this introduction, Myrna pushed her arms out at a slightly raised angle. She began to sway the arms right to left, as if she was keeping some flowing substance from touching her. Her head was tilted down, to

(30)

keep her from looking at the inevitable morass attacking her. "It's about your daughter Alexis."

"Please no. No."

"I am so sorry to have to tell you this. Your daughter has been killed this morning in her bed." Brad resisted the choking attempt in his throat. A story twice told. Once was too much. She moved past Brad, the swaying arms changed to a much slower tempo. She made her way to the sofa. She sat in an open space next to her reclining husband. She picked up his right hand and held it tight. He began to stir. The eyes fluttered open. They darted about. Looking for signs to reassure the mind, behind them, that it must have been a terrible dream. Now he could awake, and all would be normal and right. But too quickly, the eyes caught only one message. This is the real thing. Alee is gone. He looked to his weeping wife. The tragedy was real for sure. They had lost their daughter. The joy of their life. He sat up beside Myrna and pulled her close to him.

Brad; 'Folks, is there anything I can do for you?"

Edward; "No. We will be okay. I'll call Reverend Dirksen. He's our pastor. He will come and minister to us. How soon do you need us to come for the identification?" A good part of the stoicism had returned to the stricken man. He had recovered almost as quickly as he had blanked out. However, there was redness around the eyes. "One word of advice. You may want to talk to Alexis' ex-boyfriend. His name is Wade Brendon. He works for Merkle Real-estate. That's how she met him. He is the one, that sold her the house. He beat her up a few months ago and put her in the hospital. He's a brute and mean as hell."

"Yes. We have heard about him. We will definitely be talking to him."

(31)

Brad and Matt left the Struthers to grieve their loss. They were headed back to headquarters. "Jesus Brad. That was a tough assignment back there. Those folks didn't deserve this. Do you think they will be okay?"

"They seem to be tough folks. A tragedy like this is tough for anyone. I think they will pull through. Maybe not like before."

"What do you think Brad. Should we start with this Wade character?"

"Sounds like a good place to start. We'll check the data base back at the office."

Shortly after entering the station house, and a quick visit with the Captain, they headed to their desks. The Captain was filled in, on the up-to date information. Sargent Garcia had briefed the media hovering around Alexis' house. He had given the press and TV folks a short statement as to the occurrence. They were told, "that a young woman had been murdered in her bedroom, by person or persons unknown. The name of the victim was being held until next of kin notification." He asked the photographers and TV personnel not to publish or show photos of the house just yet. "The murder happened approximately seven thirty this morning. The manner in which the young lady was killed is not confirmed at this time. The body has been sent to the morgue. The Medical Examiner will be performing an autopsy. Her body was discovered by her live-in boyfriend, who had just returned to the house from a one-hour jog. There is no sign of robbery. There is no known connection to drug involvement. That is all we have for now. Check downtown tomorrow. We may have more then."

Brad and Matt began the data base run on Wade Brendon. The hit was quick. One DUI one year ago. One charge of domestic violence ten weeks ago. Plea deal on domestic violence misdemeanor. Initial charges of felony assault reduced to third degree assault misdemeanor, thirty days in the slammer. Occupation, real-estate salesman. Merkle Realty in Eugene. Two other assault charges, no prosecution, dating back two years.

"Looks like we have a brute on our hands. Likes to hit people," offered Matt.

"Yeah. A real toughie. We best go have a chat with him."

"Do you like him for the murder?"

"Well Matt, he's the first blip on the radar. But way too soon to make any assumptions."

The same old Brad, that Matt had come to respect. He was strictly a no guess man. Hunches were sometimes to be considered, but facts and discovery were the keys to nailing a perp.

Chapter 6   The Brute

Brad and Matt drove out to the Plaza across the freeway from Valley River Shopping Center. It was a small strip mall mostly occupied by real estate offices, lawyers' offices, and insurance representatives. They went into the Merkle Realty office. Brad inquired if Wade Brendon was in. The answer was no. He did not work on the weekend. He was strictly Monday through Friday. Brad asked if they had his address. He showed his ID, and informed that it was police business. The secretary gave Brad the address for Karen Morgan. She explained, that she was a friend of Wades', and Wade was staying with her. With the address in hand, Brad thanked the lady, and he and Matt departed the office.

They drove directly to the address on Parliament Street in West Eugene. There were two cars in the driveway. "Looks like somebody's home", said Matt.

At the door they were greeted by a young woman, looked to be in her early thirties. Brad introduced himself and his partner. "We are here to talk with Wade Brendon. We are told, that he resides here as your guest. Would he possibly be here just now?"

Karen looked somewhat nervous and fidgety. "Yes. Please come in. He's taking a nap in the back bedroom. I'll call him out for you." She walked down the hall and opened the bedroom door, and went in.

"Wade darling wake up. There are two police officers here. They want to talk to you."

Wade had already awoken. He was generally a very light sleeper. He actually heard the doorbell ring. He had an immediate hunch, who it most likely would be. He rolled off the bed. He was in his underwear. He grabbed

(34)

his trousers and within a minute he was dressed. It was a pullover shirt and slip-on Birkenstocks that finished off the ensemble. "Okay baby. Let's go see what they want. Just remember, I was here all morning with you."

The two friends walked down the hall and into the living room to face the officers. "Good morning officers. What can I do for you?", asked Wade.

"We are here gathering information on an Alexis Struthers. It is our understanding, that you had a recent relationship with the lady. We are told, it was you who sold her the house she was living in. We are interested in anything you can tell us about her."

Wade was wondering what else they had been told. They were sure to have the files on his domestic problem with the bitch. They had to know that he served time in the county jail over it. "You just said, the house, she was living in. That sounds like the past tense. As far as I know, she still lives there. Have you tried the house?"

Brad; "apparently you haven't heard the news this morning. Alexis was murdered in her house early this morning."

Karen gasped. Wade had not confessed anything to her about his dealings with Alexis. She shuddered. Did he have anything to do with her death? She couldn't believe, that could be the case. However, she realized that by obeying her lover, she would be perjuring herself. She felt a bit faint.

Wade flinched and ran his hand over his forehead. "I can't believe it. She was so young and vibrant. A beautiful woman. What a dirty rotten shame. I hope you catch whoever was responsible."

"Don't fret. We will, without a doubt bring the killer

(35)

to justice. Now, what can you tell us about her? How did your relationship end? Good or bad?"

"There were some complications. Some that might incriminate me. Because of that, I am going to defer any comment, until I am represented by an attorney."

"You must realize, you are a person of interest in this case. Enough so, we could bring you in."

"You do that, and you will have to file charges. What fucking charges do you have in mind?"

"You are right. However, it is in your best interest to co-operate. It could be a matter of eliminating yourself as a person of interest or even a suspect."

"Officer, I intend to co-operate fully. But like I said there are complications, that could cast a shadow on me. I will be glad to come downtown anytime. But first, I need to hire an attorney."

Brad weighed the situation in his mind. It might be a bit premature to cuff the bastard. He was right, in the issue of filing charges. Brad didn't have enough to meet that threshold. So, for now he would play the man's game. There was plenty of time to make the next move. Brad's gut feeling was, that this was suspect number one.

"We will leave it at that. One important question I would like to pose here on the spot; can you tell us your whereabouts this morning around eight thirty?"

"I know that game. One question, then another. Like I said, talk to my attorney."

"Okay. We will do it the hard way. I am arresting you for withholding information, that is tantamount to obstruction of justice. And if that is not enough, there is a charge of breaking a restraining order."

Matt read the arrestee his rights, which include the right to remain silent, as he snapped on the restraints.

"You will have the opportunity to call your lawyer, once you are booked. With all said and done, Wade was escorted into the unmarked police vehicle, and hauled downtown to the city holding pen. There, he was booked, fingerprinted, and mug shot taken. Brad knew it was premature, however, it might shake the leaves. One never knows what might fall out of the tree.

Chapter 7   Mom

After being booked in the city police department holding cell, Wade had time to weigh his options. But mostly, he sat back and reminisced about his life. His mind traced back to the day his father died. Wade was only five years old at the time. He can barely remember his father. His dad was a successful business man. That much he could remember. He was able to remember the day he was killed in an auto accident. Some crazy rich woman, driving a Cadillac, sixty miles an hour through town, ran a red light, just as dad was pulling into the intersection. He was pronounced dead at the scene. What ensued, was set indelibly in his young mind. At the funereal for his father, Aunt Gracie took him aside, and gave him a short pep talk. The part he would always remember, was when she told him, that he needed to be strong for his mother's sake. "You are now the man of the house. You need to watch out for mom."

His grief for the death of his father was short lived. A wonderous thing happened. His relationship with his mother reached new heights. She leaned on him for moral support. After weeks of grieving, she began to totally dote on her young son. They would go out to dinner, movies, and sometimes to Chucky Cheese arcade. She smothered him with her motherly warmth. She would sit and watch Scooby Doo with him on the living room sofa. She would make popcorn. She spoke wonderful things about how much she loved him. He truly felt like the king of the castle. This went smoothly for two full years. Then Blake Whitehead entered the picture. He was smooth and handsome. Mom met him at a party thrown by her sister.

They became quickly attracted to one another. Within four months they were married. Wade's world changed as quickly as the marriage was consummated.

Wade was suddenly just a child underfoot. A child with quirky moods and bad behavior. His mother became much less affectionate. She still loved her little boy. But the comradery they had shared was gone forever. 'She was just a whore.' A distinction he would assume, should be applied to all women. You most definitely could not count on their fidelity. In all the years that followed, two years in a relationship with a woman would become a barrier. That would be the time, the warranty would expire. All those ensuing relationships would inevitably end one way or another after that time frame. Generally, he would become agitated with them, and occasionally get physically rough with them. This would make them eager to break off the affair. They were all just a bunch of whores. Just like his mother. The only one that touched him more deeply was Alexis. In many ways, she reminded him of his mother. The same auburn hair and green eyes. The same perkiness. In all of that, she was the worst of the lot. She was the worst bitch of all.

Her had placed a call to his attorney. The same one, that represented him earlier in the year on the domestic charge filed by Alee. His name is Montgomery (Monty) Sinclair. He told Wade he would be in this evening to meet with him.

True to his word, Monty showed up at five thirty that same evening. "So, what's the story this time Wade? The charge sheet says obstruction of justice and violation of a restraining order. Please tell me none of it is true. And if it is, what do they mean by obstruction of justice? That generally means a serious crime has been committed."

(39)

"You probably haven't heard the news. Alexis, my ex, has been killed in her home. The cops have me here, for not wanting to discuss the matter without an attorney."

"Whoa. I did hear on the news that a young woman had been murdered this morning. I didn't tie it to Alexis. The report on the news puts the murder at seven thirty this morning. Can you, account for your time this morning? I mean if they brought you in for obstruction, that can only mean one thing. They have you high on their most likely list for the crime."

"You might say that."

"I do say that. I need to know if, you are anyway involved with the killing, either directly or indirectly. Whatever you say, is attorney-client privilege, and it can go no further than this room. That is, should you plan to retain me for any other serious charges."

"I don't plan to change horses in Mid-Gallup. If these bastards plan to drop the M bomb on me, I for sure, need you to look out for me."

"Okay. I will accept the case should it come to that. I need to know certain facts, in order to plan your defense against any charges that may be brought against you. Now, here are the rules on ethics. I am able to know, whether or not you are factually guilty. I must navigate within the system carefully with that knowledge. I cannot allow you to perjure yourself. I have to be careful in cross-examining any witness, as to their veracity. I cannot withhold any information concerning a crime, that I have knowledge of, that you are planning. Should you disclose to me, that you are guilty of any charge brought upon you, I will defend you vigorously within those guidelines. I cannot be compelled to relate any confidential information you pass to me. Legal ethics compel me not to

(40)

do so. There is substantial difference between factual guilt and legal guilt. Let's start with the restraining order. Did you violate it?"

"It was nothing. Earlier this week, I stopped by her house, to give her back a CD, I found in my stuff. I knew it was one of her favorites. I thought, I was doing the right thing. She flew off the handle, and I made tracks. End of story."

"Was there any kind of altercation? Did you raise your voice or threaten her in anyway?"

"Hell no. She was uptight and told me to leave right now. She threatened to call the police if I didn't scram. So, I scrammed. I was only there for two minutes."

"Were there any witnesses at that time?"

"There was this dude standing at the end of the hall. He could see me. I sure as hell could see him. She's already got her hooks in the asshole."

"Why do you say that?"

"You can tell when someone has been humping someone else. They have that smug look. That moon struck look. Like they are someone really special. Whores have a way to pull that kind of shit off."

"Did it make you mad, seeing another man with your old girlfriend?"

"Hell. I just felt sorry for the dumb prick. I knew she would turn him inside out. My bet is, he snuffed her."

"Here are some more rules. Do not repeat anything you have said to me just now. Do not talk to anyone here in the jail, unless I am present. Especially, do not talk to anyone from the media. Do not talk to the police. Do not talk to other inmates. You understand? I will talk to the release desk. I should be able to get you released without security. You may have to appear Monday morning for a

(41)

plea hearing. My guess is, they will drop the charges. It was most likely a kneejerk action, that got you in here in the first place. By the way, can you, account, for your whereabouts this morning at seven thirty?"

"That I can do. I was home with Karen all morning, until the cops showed up."

Monty left the cell and approached the sergeant at the release desk in an office towards the front of the building.

"What's the story on my client, Wade Brendon? Do you have him rated for an easy out? The charge sheet looks pretty thin and there doesn't appear to be any warrant."

"He's being held on two charges. A violation of restraining order, and failure to co-operate with authorities in a murder investigation, in which he is a primary person of interest. I can't release him until he's had his first appearance before a judge. He's set for nine AM Monday morning."

"So, you are going to make me do it the hard way. You know, that these are small fry claims. I'll have to roust a judge out of his weekend relaxation to get a writ for release."

"I suggest you talk to the arresting officer. Detective Brad Ferguson. He has the authority to give recommendation for preliminary release. If you like I can buzz him."

"Get him out here. Let's get this charade settled."

Brad happened to be working in his office late, due to the Struthers' case. He answered the sergeant's buzz and came into the release office. "You called?"

(42)

"The arrest you made today, is looking for a get out of jail pass. This is his attorney."

Brad looked Monty in the eye. "You have a bad boy for a client. We have him charged primarily for violation of a restraining order. A violation, that occurred but a couple of days, before the subject, of the restraining order was violently murdered in her own bed. In our investigation of that murder, your client refused to co-operate on basic information. If you are willing to have your client answer some very routine questions, it could result in our dropping that charge. Obviously, we would not have the ability, to take testimony from the victim of the broken restraining order, inasmuch as, she is also the victim of homicide. You're here. I'm here. It should only take ten or fifteen minutes."

"My client has nothing to hide. He will be forthright, and answer your questions, under my guidance. I need to know, if you have any other charges up your sleeve."

"No. What you see is what you get. Unless of course, he wants to confess to some criminal activity."

The interrogation was held in an office set up for questioning. A recorder was placed on the table. Brad sat across the table from the defendant and his counsel." This interview will be recorded." Brad read the date and time into the recorder and named all present.

"Mr. Brendon, you are aware that your ex-girlfriend, Alexis Struthers, was murdered early this morning?"

"I am. You related that fact to me at my residence earlier today."

"What was your relationship with her as of today, before her demise?"

Monty; "We will pass on that question. You may ask if my client had any ill feelings toward the victim."

Brad; "I'll pass on that one. We know, by court records, that your client had major problems with the lady. I'll get to the point. Can you, account for your whereabouts at seven thirty this morning?"

Monty whispered in Wade's ear, "Be precise and do not elaborate."

Wade; "I was at Karen Morgan's home. I hang my hat there. I was there all morning, until you came and whisked me away."

"Was Karen with you the whole time between six thirty and eight O'clock this morning?"

"Yes, she was."

"Did you go to Alexis' home earlier this week, and confront her at the front door of her home?"

Again, the whisper in the ear. "Yes, I did."

"Did you not realize that you were violating a court order in doing so?"

"Yes, I do. I was returning a music CD of hers, that ended up in my stuff when we split. I figured she would want it back."

"Apparently you do not have much regard for a court order. Did you still have strong feelings for Alexis, after your breakup?"

"We had some good times together. I regret that I treated her badly. I tried to make it up to her. Do I still have strong feelings for her? I would say that I held her in high regard. I am devastated by her sudden death."

Monty addressed Brad; "You need to declare here and now, if you are looking at Wade, as a potential suspect in the death of the victim. He has not yet been charged in that respect. I believe my client has answered forthrightly your questions. If your only remaining charge is the court order violation, you should be aware, I have already

(44)

checked records, and find that, apparently the victim did not file any restraining order violation. If you have information contrary to that, you are compelled by law to disclose that to me. For now, I am requesting you to advise the release desk, and have them allow for his release. I will guarantee his reporting for any court hearing."

Brad considered the matter for a few seconds and gave his reply. "I see no harm in that. We will maintain his status as a person of interest in the homicide investigation. He can walk for now. Sign the papers at the desk, which will include a citation for appearance Monday morning on the restraint violation, Circuit Court room 3, at nine AM. And counselor, I wouldn't count too much on the victim's failure to file the violation. I will tell you here and now, we have an eye witness to the infraction. The court does not look kindly on those breaking court orders."

Chapter 8   Big Brother Comes to Town

Robert checked into the Hilton Hotel in the middle of town. He was assigned room 315. He unloaded his luggage on the coffee table in a cove adjacent to the bedroom. He refreshed himself in the bathroom. He watered down a hand towel and rubbed it across his forehead. He sat down in an armchair in the bedroom. He pulled out his cell-phone and punched in the contact button for his brother, Steve. It was now a few minutes before nine. "Stevio, I am glad I caught you. I've got some really terrible news to lay on you."

"Christ. Are you okay? Has there been an accident?

"No. Nothing like that. I'm fine. It's about Alexis. She was murdered in her bed at home, just this morning, about two hours ago."

"Oh my god. That is terrible. Do the police know who the killer is? Has there been any arrest?"

"Not that I know of. Her ex-boyfriend is a person of interest, as they put it. I guess you could say, that I am also a person of interest. Seeing as how, I was staying at her house, and was most likely the last person to see, and talk to her except for the killer."

"Are they putting any pressure on you? Have you contacted an attorney? You shouldn't be talking to the police without counsel."

"I have co-operated so far. They want me at the station Monday morning for a deposition, or interview. I figure on calling for an attorney first thing Monday morning. I may have to stick around for a while. I certainly want to be here for the services. I would like to stick around and see what develops in the case."

"Little brother, I will catch a flight tomorrow and meet you there. Two heads are better than one. Sometimes, police have ways of tripping suspects up. Don't tell me any more over the phone. Save it for tomorrow."

"Jeeze Steve. I think I can handle it. After all, I am totally innocent. And I don't have any information that will be of much use for them."

"Don't sweat it. I'll be there. You and I have got to stick together as always."

Robert could tell by the tone in his brother's voice, that there was no way, that he was not going to be on that plane tomorrow. "Call me when, you know what time you will be in. I will pick you up."

Steve arrived Sunday morning at eleven AM. Robert was there to meet him, and ferry him back to the Hilton. Robert had rented a Toyota from Hertz the day before. The hotel was confining, and he felt the need to drive around the area. It was also handy for retrieving his brother from the airport Sunday morning. "How was the flight?"

"Right on time. Nothing to it. So, what's our agenda?"

"Let's check you in the hotel. I only have one bed. I'm sure you will want room to stretch out in. After you get settled, we can have lunch in the hotel restaurant."

"Sounds good. You can fill me in at the hotel. So, this is Eugene, Oregon. All I know about the town is they have a fine university. Hell, of a football program."

Steve checked into the third floor, a couple of doors down from Robert's room. After depositing his luggage and use of the facilities, he buzzed room 315. "Why don't you come on over to my room? I have plenty of space to spread out."

(47)

The brothers met in Steve's room. "Now give me the details on everything. Start with how you met her, on from there up to date."

Robert told his brother the whole story. The initial meeting, his decision to come to Eugene in order to extend the relationship. How she met him at the airport. The trip to the Oregon coast. How wonderful she had been. He mentioned Wade coming to the house, and Alexis explaining the busted relationship. "He had beaten her pretty bad. She had to go to emergency. She filed charges. He spent thirty days in jail and was slapped with a restraining order to stay away from her."

"Well, I must say, that makes him look to be a possible suspect. I'm sure there were some ill feelings there."

"I mentioned that to the police. He didn't look very happy when he came to her door. She ordered him to leave immediately, or she would call the police. He scrammed. I think the police will be talking to him."

"Let's talk about you. You say you were jogging and she was still in bed. You've said, that the police put the time of death at approximately seven thirty. And you say that is about the time you left the house. That could be a serious time line, putting you at the scene at about the time of the murder."

"Yeah. I understand all of that. All I know for sure, is that I didn't do it."

"I have no doubt about that. But we have to be realistic.
We have to think how the police and the law would put things together. There has been more than one innocent person tried and convicted, for a crime they did not commit. You could be facing serious charges.

(48)

The first thing in the morning, we have got to find you a good attorney. One thing I am sure of, is that, you must keep your story line precise. Do not get tangled up and misspeak. If they think you are changing your story in anyway, it could lead them to think you are lying and trying to cover up."

"I don't see that happening. My story is the unadulterated truth. There are no complications at all."

"I'll buy that. Let's get some lunch, then maybe you can show me the town."

Chapter 9   Assassination

Karen had a fitful morning Saturday. What was with Wade? Did he kill his old girlfriend? Was she to be an accomplice by lying to the police about his being at home all morning? How could she handle this? Perhaps make hasty trip out of town. She knew how brutish Wade could be. 'Perhaps fiendish enough to kill. Where does that put me. If he did in fact kill Alexis, why not me. I know I can't cross him. Way too dangerous.'

In the end, Karen decided to wait it out. If they keep him in jail, it would give her more time to sort out her actions. This would not be the case. That evening he arrived back at her house. His attorney had driven him home. She was filled with dread, the moment he entered the door. His first words were, "We need to talk."

"Yes dear. I think we do need to talk. You must tell me, what in hell is going on?"

"It's simple but complicated. First of all, get it out of your head, that I had anything to do with Alexis' murder. That part is the simple part. The complicated part is, that I had a business meeting with some partners. It is a meeting, I do not intend for the police to know anything about. It was a meeting concerning illegal transactions. Keep it under your hat, I am a middle man for drug trafficking. It would be more than dangerous for me, for it to leak out. The people I deal with do not like publicity of any sort. My position is acting as an agent for suppliers. I don't traffic to the public. I simply make drops to the various dealers in the area. Sorta like wholesale."

"Isn't that legal if you have a license?"

"Only for pot. I'm not talking about pot."

"Wade, that's shocking. I had no idea, you were being a criminal. That puts me in a bad spot. If they get onto you, won't they tie me into it as well?"

"That's why darling, they must not get onto me. Things go on as normal. I make good money on this job. I've got plenty saved up. We can bust out of here and do some serious traveling."

"Wade, I love you dearly, but this is too much for me. I think we should split up. That would make things less complicated for you. I would just be a chain around your neck. You know how nervous I get when cross-examined."

They were setting on the living room sofa. Wade got up of the couch and grabbed her by the arm. He pulled her abruptly off the seat, and slapped her hard across the face. He yanked her hair from the back and put his face close to hers. "Don't be a bitch. You will do as I say, or I'll kick your ass so hard you'll be walking on all fours for a month."

Karen broke out in tears and began sobbing audibly. "Yes Wade. I'll do as you say. Please don't hurt me."

Monday morning Wade was dressed and ready to go to court. He stepped out the front door and was walking towards his car, when three gunshots busted the morning quietness. The shots came from a car parked close to his driveway. The three shots found their target. He was hit three times. The one that killed him instantly had pierced his heart. It had happened so fast, that Wade had no time to understand, that he was breathing his last breath. No goodbyes dear world. No remorse. No nothing. The car carrying the shooter drove away without haste. It was soon out of the neighborhood. No witnesses were there to take notes.

Karen had heard the shots fired. She was sure they were gunshots, and not some errant backfiring

(51)

automobile. She went to her door and opened it, as she took a step outside. Not far from her position, she saw Wade lying on the driveway. He had not made it to his car. He would not make it to his court date. He would not be slapping her around anymore. She felt that she should be filled with remorse. But, that was not the sentiment that filled her just now. All she could feel, was that somebody had just solved all of her problems. From the look of the scene, he was surely dead. She went over and knelt beside him There was much blood. He was lying face down. She felt his wrist for a pulse. There was none. There was no one on the street. She went back inside and called 911.

Within minutes, there were squad cars pulling up to the driveway. An ambulance also arrived quickly. She was questioned by a young officer. She told, what she could; that Wade was on his way to a court hearing. He was walking towards his car when shots rang out. She stepped out when she heard the gunfire, and found Wade on the ground. She had checked his pulse, and when none was detected, she ran back inside and called 911.

That same Monday morning, Robert and Steve had called a local attorney, and made an early morning appointment to meet. The firm was Middleton and Jacobs. The attorney was William Jacobs. The meeting was in the office's conference room. It was a rather ornate affair, with a large table that could seat a dozen. The three men sat at one end of the table. Mr. Jacobs sat at the end one side, and the brothers sat side by side directly across the table from the attorney.

"Gentlemen, your call sounded rather urgent. You say that you need assistance in making a report to the local police involving a homicide. Tell me about it."

(52)

Robert; "It's like this. I met this lady in San Jose, where I reside. We hit it off pretty good, and we both agreed that I should come here to visit. Last Saturday, I flew up from California and we hooked up. For me, it was love at first sight. I think it was reciprocal. Like I said, we hit it off pretty good. I stayed with her all week. Early Saturday morning, I went for a jog leaving her in bed. When I got back an hour later, she was still in bed. She was not alive. Somebody had killed her while I was out on my run. I checked for a pulse. There wasn't any. I called 911 and reported the situation. I was interviewed by Detective Ferguson from Eugene Police. It was a short interview, as I was shaken up by finding Alexis dead. I mean, I had just spoken to her an hour earlier. The detective asked me to come to the station this morning for my deposition."

William; "I see. Can you tell me word for word what you released to the detective?"

"Yes, I think so. It wasn't much different than what I have just told you. I did tell him, that he might want to check on her ex-boyfriend, Wade Brendon. They had a bad breakup. He beat her and went to jail for it. She had a restraining order, which he
violated earlier in the week by coming to her door. She was angry at him, and told him to leave immediately or she would call the police."

"Did he leave immediately?"

"Yes. But he looked upset and angry himself. He saw me standing in the hall. I don't think it went over well."

"I have heard of the case. I must ask, did you have any hand in her death? Whatever you reply, it is protected by attorney-client privilege. I have agreed to take your case. I need to know as much as I can, to guide you through the interview downtown."

(53)

"I absolutely did not. I loved the lady and was ready to propose."

"Okay. I'll take that on faith. Now, we must persuade the police to believe you as well. I will ask for the detective's notes from his first interview with you, before we proceed with further interrogation. I will I need to learn, if they are considering you as a possible suspect. Are you now ready to proceed to the police?"

"As ready as I will ever be."

With this interview completed, the three man drove to police headquarters. Once inside, William asked to see Detective Ferguson. The time was ten AM. The detective had just recently returned from the Wade Brendon murder scene. He was discussing the new case with his partner Matt Wagner in their office. He went out to the reception area and met with the trio. He knew quite a bit about the lawyer with the two brothers. He had a solid reputation as defense counsel in high profile cases. In a way, he was glad that Robert had sought good representation. His gut feeling was that Robert had got caught up in an ugly situation. His intuition told him the man was not complicit in the murder. However, every now and then, one gets blindsided. He couldn't let his gut feelings dictate his own course of action. At any rate, he was pleased to see Jacobs on the job. "Good morning gents. Please follow me into the interview room."

Inside the interrogation room the four men became acquainted. "William how are you doing these days? I see you are still practicing. I take it, you are here to represent Robert in these proceedings. I will tell you up front that your client is not at this time a suspect in the Homicide of Alexis Struthers. He is merely a person of interest in the

(54)

investigation. Seeing as how he discovered the body. I am certain, that he advised you on our first interview at the scene."

"Detective Ferguson, yes he has. Before we answer any further questions, I would ask to see the notes you have concerning that earlier interview."

"Not a problem. I have them here. Please take your time in going over them."

William studied the handwritten note Brad had jotted down as he had interviewed Robert at the residence. Once satisfied with his perusal, the interrogation began. The interview was short, and William had no need to cut in or advise his client on any issue raised by the detective. Then came the issue of the sudden death of Wade Brendon. "Robert, are you aware of the murder this morning of Wade Brendon?"

"Wow. That was sudden for sure. This is definitely the first I have heard. You did say murder? Is that for sure?"

"As sure as daylight. He was shot down in the driveway at the house he was staying in. It happened about eight thirty this morning. He was on his way to court for a hearing on the restraint violation. Now I must ask you, if you can verify where you were at that time?"

William turned to his client and whispered in his ear. He then turned to Brad, and interjected that his client was at the Hilton having breakfast at that time.

"Was there anyone with you at that time?"

"I was alone. Steve passed on breakfast. He's not a breakfast person."

"How long of a time were the two of you separated this morning?"

"Maybe forty minutes."

(55)

"This is important. Did you have any contact with Wade, since Alexis' murder?"

"Absolutely not."

"However, you did harbor bad ill towards the man?"

William, "There has been no indication that my client held any bad ill towards your latest victim. He barely knew the man, and that would be indirectly. Please keep your questions based on factual information. Keep your speculations out of this interview. Gather your findings and take them to the DA."

Detective Ferguson; "Robert, that is all for now. You are free to travel out of our jurisdiction. I will ask that you keep us informed of your whereabouts. You are now a person of interest in both homicides. We may very likely need to call you
in, as this case progresses. I would ask that you keep your attorney advised whenever you travel. It would not be a good idea to leave the country."

Robert, his brother, and attorney rode together back to William's office. They held a short conference and signed a client agreement for the law firm. Robert paid a retainer and gave all the pertinent information as to his home address and workplace. He told the attorney he would be in town for the remainder of the week. He had already confirmed with Alexis' parents about the services, which would be held Saturday.

Upon departing the law office, Steve queried his brother about what his plans were.

"I think I may be taking a short leave of absence. I would like to stick around, and see how this thing plays out. I appreciate your coming here. You've been a great support as always. I may be able to console Alee's folks. I

(56)

know they are suffering as much and more than I am. Anyway, maybe my being close will give them some comfort."

"I read you little brother. Just be careful. Don't talk to the police without William at your side. Be sure to call me if anything breaks. I'll go ahead and take the afternoon flight back to San Jose. Remember I'm only a phone call away. I can be back here in a flash. The 'Centurion' project, your team is working on should be able to struggle ahead for a while. Sooner or later they will need you on the job. It will be a great day for the company when that baby is wrapped. The military is licking their chops since we gave them a preview of the project. We won a few chips with the pentagon, when we delivered 'Eagle Eyes' to them. All reports so far are 100% positive. The company has you to thank for that project."

"I'm happy how that one worked out. Of course, I never had any doubts. And it gives a leg up on the 'Centurion' project. The company doesn't owe me any thanks. The bonus covered that item quite nicely."

"Yes. But just you wait. 'Centurion' will make you richer than you can imagine. An absolute anti-missile defense system that can knock down any type of missile, short range or inter-continental is a world changer. You best, buy more company stock."

"Steve, I'll let you worry about the money. I can always hit you up for a loan." They both chuckled.

Chapter 10   Other Players

Tuesday morning at the Eugene Police Department, Brad and Matt were in their joint office talking over the two recent homicides, when Detective Sergeant Alan Prebilsky came into the room. Alan is a tall stoutly built man of Polish decent, with looks that could have made him a movie idol. He was the type of man, that would draw much attention from the young ladies that encountered him. He had that outdoors look. He was respected by his peers for his diligence and focus. He did his job with sincere objectivity. He was in short, a damn good detective. He carried himself well and displayed a stern air of authority. Today he is assigned as liaison agent to work with the local DEA. It's a tour, he has been on for the last two years.

"Brad, Matt, good morning. Have you got a few moments?"

"Good morning to you Al. What's on your mind?"

"I may have some items of interest that might touch on your investigation of the Wade Brendon murder."

Brad; "That so. Pray tell, what have you got?"

"As you know I have been assigned to co-operate with DEA for the last couple of years. Your victim, Brendon was on their list. He has been under scrutiny for the last several weeks. They think, he was involved with drug trafficking in our area. They were building a case, when the shit hit the fan. He is linked with the Ferrell Brothers in Venita. The brothers have been on the radar for the last several months. That is how they picked up on Brendon. He has been observed making frequent trips out to Venita. I have here a dossier of him meeting the brothers at their house in Venita. Photos will show him delivering something to them in tote bags. We are pretty sure the bags contained contraband. DEA had gathered enough for probable cause warrant. We were in the stage of planning a bust. Brendon's murder makes it imperative that the bust goes down. It might be a shake of the dice, whether or not they are holding contraband just now. But the best guess, is they are in possession. I wanted to clue you in. We might want to see, if there is a tie-in to the murder."

Brad; "That's for damn sure. Something to chew on for certain. Let's look at your files."

Al opened up the vanilla folder and spread out several photographs. They showed Wade driving his BMW in the Venita area. Venita is a small community, 20 miles west of Eugene on Hwy 126, highway to Florence on the coast. There were photos of Wade carrying a satchel from his parked car to the Ferrell brother's house. There were file reports on the brothers. Mostly small charges concerning rowdy behavior and criminal mischief. Multiple tips taken on the street, which put term on DEA radar. There was reports printed out on Wade Brendon. His domestic problems were in the report as well as the prior DUI. Nothing regarding illegal substance possession.

Brad; "So, Al, you have a hunch that the brothers may have had a falling out with their source. You like them for snuffing Brendon."

"Less crazy outcomes than that occur frequently. I think it's worth exploring. It could be as simple as a drug deal gone sour."

Brad; "We may have one lead to check out. Wade was living with a lady named Karen Morgan. She might be able to shed some light on her boyfriend's activities. She was to be his alibi for the Saturday morning killing. We

(59)

haven't grilled her yet. This may be the right time to visit her."

Al; "I would like to come long for that interview. If that sets okay with you."

"Three dickheads are better than two." Brad chuckled. "We better track her on the phone and make sure she can meet us. She works for Merkle Realty. That's where she met Brendon."

The quick phone call to Merkle's was positive. Karen was indeed on the job. She was put on the line. "This is Karen. Can I help you?"

Brad advised Karen that he needed to meet with her in regards to her friend's death. She replied that she could get out of the office on a break. "I will be at the house in fifteen minutes."

The three officers drove to Karen's, and arrived simultaneously as she pulled up. They got out of their car and joined Karen at the front door. "Please come in."

They walked into the house and into the living room. Brad introduced Allen. She had already met Brad and Matt. "We have just a few questions to ask. "First, I need to know if Wade was with you all morning last Saturday?"

Karen had no compunction now to lie. There would be no repercussions for her telling the truth. Not now. She had been spared having to tell the lie in the first place. This was the first time it was put to her. "The answer to that is no. Wade went out early Saturday and was gone for at least an hour."

"Did he ask you to lie to us about that?"

"Yes. And if I didn't he would kick my butt. He could be mean that way."

Brad, "Did he give you any answer, as to where he was that morning?"

"His story to me was that he had a business meeting. A meeting he could not give out to the police. I think it had something to do with drugs."

Allen; "Brad if you don't mind, I would like to follow up on that."

"Shoot."

"Karen, can you give us any information on Wade trafficking in controlled substance? Did you ever observe any drugs in his possession? Did he ever try to pass any on to you?"

"No. I swear I never saw anything like that. He did carry a tote bag quite often coming and going. I never questioned about it. He never offered any drugs to me. You can test me. I never touch anything like that."

"Is the tote bag in the house now? If so, do you mind if we pick it up?"

"He usually kept it in the spare bedroom closet. You can check. If it's there, feel free to take it."

Karen was being very co-operative. She appeared to be clean of any activities, that Wade was involved in. Matt and Allen went to the spare bedroom, Karen pointed out. They returned to the living room with a black plastic tote bag.

Brad; "Karen, you told us Monday, that when you stepped outside, you did not observe any vehicles or pedestrians. Please think hard. Try to recall, if there was any car traveling up the street at that time." Karen sat on the sofa and visibly attempted to recall the scene.

"I do sorta of remember a sand colored car. But, it was far up the street. I didn't give it much thought. I was stricken by the bloody scene of Wade lying there on the pavement. I ran back in the house and called 911 right away."

(61)

Allen; "Did Wade ever mentioned any names of the people he was dealing with?"

Karen; "No. The only thing he told me, was that he did not deal with the public. He was some sort of in-between man for distributors and pushers. He called it wholesaling. This all came up when he wanted me to lie about his being home that morning. He swore to me, it had nothing to do with Alexis. He claimed he had nothing to do with that. I think he knew, I would never cover for him in a murder. He was a suspect, wasn't he?"

Brad; "He was on our list. However, we have no tangible proof. Hopefully, we will piece it together in time. Now let me ask you about Wade. Did he have any enemies you know about? Did he ever have friends over to the house? Did the two of you socialize with anyone that made you uncomfortable?"

"Honestly I cannot think of anyone that would want to harm Wade. He was very friendly and jovial. He was sweet to me unless something riled him. He was pretty quick with a slap to the face where I was concerned. You must think, I'm pretty dumb to take it. Please understand, that sort of thing hadn't happened for the first several weeks. It shocked me. I learned later that he had beaten Alexis. From then on, I was too terrified to cross him. I did suggest that we split last Saturday. I really did not relish the idea of lying to the police. But, when I asked to split up, he got mad, and slapped me a couple of times. He yanked my hair real hard. With his face close to mine, he swore he would kick the holy you know what out me, if I didn't play ball."

Brad; "Well you need not worry on that account anymore. He won't be bothering you again. You take care.

(62)

If anyone else contacts you about Wade, I mean anybody, please contact me at this number. Day or night." Brad handed Karen his official business card with his cell-phone number.

Karen accepted the card. "I can tell you, that I believe, Wade really had ill feelings towards Alexis. I think he still had the hots for her. At the same time, I think, he hated her. Like she double crossed him or something."

Brad; "That would explain a lot. Feel free to stop by the station anytime you need to talk. And no. We don't think you are dumb. Many women get caught up in an affair, that sometimes goes sideways. I know, it can sometimes become a trap, hard to get untangled from. Especially when the guy turns out to be a thug." The detectives left Karen and headed back to the shop.

In the car, Matt pondered how could a nice young lady like Karen get herself in such a messy affair.

Brad; "Shit happens to nice people too damn often."

Chapter 11   Grieving

After driving Steve to the airport and waving him off, Robert went back to the hotel downtown. It was Monday evening. Robert decide to have dinner away from the hotel. He enjoyed Mexican food, and found an advertisement for the 'Ranchito' in Springfield. The ad read homemade flour tortillas. A rarity these days. It was certainly worth a try.

The restaurant was typically decked out in Mexican décor. It was rather large. Looked to be able to seat over two hundred. It appeared clean and the aromas were beckoning. It had been a good call. Not only were the tortillas marvelous, rolled around a shredded beef taco filling, but the margaritas were well constructed. This was a dinner that would be well enjoyed, and to followed by a Cuesta Rey back at the hotel in the back patio.

Robert had finished his evening meal and cigar by eight PM. He sat in his room and reflected on the typhoon of events. He thought of Alexis. He lamented that that she was no more. He would not have the pleasure of her adoring company. He turned his thoughts to her mother and father. He planned to go to her services Saturday. But he should visit the folks, and see if they need anything from him. He picked up his cell-phone and called their number. Edward answered the call.

"What is it Robert?"

"I just wanted you to know I am still here. I will be at the services Saturday. I thought, I might could pick you and Myrna up and drive you there. And when you are up to it, I would like very much to come over and visit with you. I know how much pain you ae going through. It has hit me pretty hard as well."

The Struthers had agreed with Robert, as to his coming by. It was set for Wednesday morning at ten. He rang their door at five till. Edward answered the door. "Good morning Robert. We are so glad to have you drop by."

"I'm happy you could take time to visit with me. The world is very gloomy just now. I miss Alee very much. I didn't get near enough time to enjoy her life. What little I did get to share, will always be precious to me."

Edward; "Robert, we are all very sad. It is a tragic loss to each of us. Alexis was a bright, beautiful woman. She enjoyed life, and that love of life, was contagious to others around her. The man that killed her was a beast. I don't have any idea how people can become that way. To take the life of a vibrant, beautiful person with no sign of conscious. To bring misery to so many. I can only find peace, knowing the monster will harm no others. Whoever shot him down, did us all a great favor."

"You sound as if you are one hundred percent sure it was Wade, that murdered Alee."

"One hundred percent." The look on Edwards face, contributed to express his certainty, that Wade was the killer, and the world had been set partially right by his death.

"I hope you are right Ed. It would be good for closure's sake. An end to the nightmare."

Myrna entered the living room and greeted Robert with a warm hug and smile. "How are you Robert? Holding up okay?"

"I'm doing the best I can. It is going to take time."

"Yes. It is going to take a lot of time. Can I get you something to drink? Iced tea, lemonade, or a soda?"

(65)

"I never turn down lemonade, thank you." Myrna turned and walked towards the kitchen.

Ed; "She is a fine woman. Strong and right with the Lord. Are you a believer, Robert?"

Robert was sorry, Ed had asked that question. This didn't seem like a proper time to go into theological sparring. "I'm afraid not really. You see, I am a scientist, and that makes for conflict on biblical leanings."

Edward. "It really shouldn't. There are many things that science cannot allow for. But I won't try to convert you. Let me just say that all life is driven towards the future. Or you might say pulled towards it. I think of life as a gigantic ocean. We are all adrift in that ocean. Ahead of each of us, is a large powerful ship. Those of us that have procreated and bore children, have them on that ship. They hold a towline that is attached to our own individual small powerless craft. It is they, that will tow us into the future. If there is only one child, as in our case, and that child perishes, there is no towline to pull us into the centuries ahead. However, there is another towline that pulls us in another direction by another line holder. This line is held by the Lord. Everyone is allowed to be towed. Everyone has a towline inside them. All they have to do is throw their line out to him. The Lord will catch every line thrown to him, and tow the small craft that he is floating in, all the way to the heavenly shore. All that is required from the drifting person is to keep the line tight. Do not let too much slack gather. That could result in aimlessly drifting. Never make it to heaven that way. It becomes much easier when you have a good partner sharing the faith. Two people, to make sure the tow line is tight and strong. I have that with Myrna. Together, we keep a tight hold on the rope."

(66)

Myrna re-entered the room carrying a tray with three sparkling iced lemonades. She motioned the tray in front of Robert. He picked up the offered glass with a thank you. She offered the tray to Edward. They each had a beverage in their hand. Robert sipped the tangy sweet concoction. They each sipped as they chatted.

Myrna; "Bob, will you be going home after the services?"

Bob; "I thought, I might stay in town for a short while. I want to be sure Alee's case is finalized."

Myrna; "Oh Bob. Don't you think it's over? I mean, with Wade dead and all."

"I know it looks that way. I would rather, it had been adjudicated by the courts. Can we be sure it was Wade?"

Ed: "Robert, you can rest assured it was Wade. There is no other plausible explanation."

Robert stayed with the Struthers for another two hours. They decided it would be nice of Bob to pick them up Saturday.

Chapter 12   Incriminating Evidence

Tuesday morning, Karen had just taken her morning shower. She had taken the rest of the week off from work. She had so much re-adjustment to do. She was unable to mourn for Wade. She was feeling sorry that she had ever met him. The fact she had given herself to him seemed demeaning now. There seemed to have been a monster inside of him. She hoped to be able to put the entire affair far behind her.

After breakfast, she began to go through his things. His clothes in the closet and drawers. In rounding things together, she came across his Sony pocket-sized camera. She sat on the side of the bed and toyed with the camera. She selected the photo album button and began to view his stored photographs. Close to the very front, she was shocked to see the picture taken of Alexis. It was a photo taken of Alexis in her bed. She was propped up on two pillows, with the view exposing her breasts. The face had a far-away look. An unnatural look. A lifeless look. Karen gasped.

There was only one course of action. She dressed and grabbed the camera. She went to her car and drove to the Eugene Police Station. Inside the building, Karen asked the receptionist if she could see Detective Ferguson.

Within two minutes, Brad was in the foyer and greeted Karen. "What brings you here, Karen?"

"This." She handed the camera to Brad. "You need to look at Wade's stored images. There is one of Alexis. I think it was taken of her, as she lay dead in her bed."

"Come on back to my office. We need to check it out."

Back in Brad's office Matt was sitting at his desk adjacent to Brad's. "Good morning Karen. How are you this fine morning?"

"Good morning officer Wagner. I'm good. I just came down to give you folks Wade's camera. It has a spooky photo saved in it. I thought it might be important."

Brad had the camera in his hand. He worked the saved image function, and the gallery was opened. Right up front, was the picture in question. "I'll be hogtied. Look at this Matt. It looks like Wade wanted a souvenir."

Matt perused the photo on the small screen. "Well, I guess, this ties up the who done-it in the Struthers' file."

Brad; "I don't see any other explanation. Karen, do you mind if we keep this camera for evidence. I want the DA to see it. After they are finished with it, you will be able to retrieve it. I'm afraid, it makes Wade to be the murderer of Alexis. That image on the camera, is exactly as Alexis was found Saturday morning. Right down to the finest detail."

"You can have it. I have no need or want of it. My quest in life is to get as far away from Wade as possible. It will take some time. I am so glad that I never had to lie for him. The way things were, I have to admit, I probably would have. It would have made me complicit in his crime."

Brad; "Don't knock yourself out. You were under extreme pressure. You were just another victim of a terrible man."

Brad met with his captain and explained the evidence on Wade's camera. "Okay Brad. Shoot it over to the prosecutors. Make hard copies for our files. You have positive ownership of the camera?"

(69)

Brad; "I would say so. His current girlfriend found it in his items, stored at her home. She positively identified it as belonging to Wade. I think that's material enough, wouldn't you say?"

"It passes the test. We can at least close the file on the Struthers' murder. Now you've got to uncover the second murder. Do you suppose it ties into the girl's murder?"

"That's always a possibility. However, Sergeant Prebilsky has been working with the DEA, and there is another possible. It appears, Mr. Brendon was working courier for some drug traffickers. His death could conceivably be tied to a drug misunderstanding. Those things sometimes occur."

"Stay on it. Keep me posted."

Brad had hard copies printed off the camera photo-card. He replaced the card in the camera and hand delivered it to the Deputy DA, that had been assigned to the Struthers' case. The deputy's response, on reviewing the hard copy and the small review screen on the camera, was, "Pretty convincing, that whoever took the shot perpetrated the homicide. Since the perp is deceased, we will close the file, with Wade Brendon materially identified as the suspect. He was high on our list of who done it. Were he still alive, and with this evidence in hand, it would have been a tight case. The case will be closed on that note. Thanks Brad, for saving us time and work on this one."

Chapter 13   The Ferrell Brothers

David, Frank, and Morgan Ferrell are three brothers living in the Venita area west of Eugene. David is the eldest and Morgan is the youngest. Frank, go figure. They are separated in age, by a mere year and a half between the eldest and the next in line. The same separation is true for the second and third. As teenagers they became a problem for mom and dad. They were constantly getting into some scrap or another. Mom's sister Jane, became the release valve. Jane's husband of twenty-five years, had been taken in a fatal driving accident. His blood-alcohol at the time of the crash was 2.4. Three times the state allowance for drivers. Fortunately, the crash was a single car accident. He had driven off the road, down an embankment and rolled hard against a tree. He had been pronounced dead at the scene.

Jane had always enjoyed the three nephews. She felt they were, in her own words, 'merely over stimulated.' When things got too hot at her sister's home, with the boys being more rebellious than ever, a family meeting concluded that the boys would move out to Venita, and live with their aunt. She was a bit lonely with the loss of her husband two years earlier. She was also very fond of the three youths. And her house was plenty big enough for the group. The general thinking was, that the boys might settle down out in the country. Venita is a small community with a very rural atmosphere. David had turned eighteen, and by a miracle, had graduated from high school. The miracle being, it took three transfers over the course of four years, from one school mishap to another. These mishaps, for the most part, were of the rowdiness behavior nature. Some included destruction of school property. His saving grace was a quick and bright mind. With little effort, he was able to master his courses and attain passing status. The school was happy to pass him on and out.

The remaining two brothers had a very slim outlook for any scholastic achievement. They were most likely, to go through life with an eighth-grade education. All three boys had taken up pot in their early teens. Eventually, they began to experiment with other illegal substances. There was a period of time, that methamphetamine was easily available.

In 2011, Aunt Jane passed away from pancreatic cancer. She suffered for three months in agony before finally ending her suffering with a gasping moan. The nephews had been very attentive to her in her final months. They cared for her night and day. In this, there was some mercy for her. She was continually surrounded by the three young men, that meant so much to her. She could not have wished for better loving care. The boys were deeply traumatized by her ordeal and final passing. They had formed a closer bond with Jane, than they would ever duplicate in the future with any other human. She had been like an older sister, and at times like a mother. She was their shield against the outside world.

Jane had left the boys equally, to share in her assets. Primarily the house in Venita. There was in addition to the house, a savings account, with a staggering amount of two hundred and eighty thousand dollars. It was this dowry that enabled the boys to go into business. That business was soon catapulted by their meeting with Wade Brendon. The upstart business was in the trafficking of illegal substance. Wade had developed as a supplier of Heroin,

(72)

cocaine, meth, marijuana, and opioids. He became a constant supplier of these goods. The brothers would be his main clients. They had no contact with the main supplier. Wade was the man. His connection in San Diego, was the source for funneling the drugs north. Once a month, a mule would deliver the contraband to Wade at a set location in the Eugene area.

It had been a lucrative proposition. Pot had recently become less attractive, due to the state legalizing recreational marijuana. It was being sold on practically every street corner. The state was suddenly enjoying a new and healthy tax revenue. The police were faced with new challenges regarding what constituted DUI. One of the notorious effects of weed, is that the THCs stay in the body long after lighting up. State statutes almost allow for smoking while driving. It is treated as a misdemeanor with a fine of $280. However, if the driver is tested for disorientation and found to be impaired, then it becomes a DUI. This would be treated by law, much the same as alcohol.

The thriving Ferrell Brother's drug operation was bolstered by meth and heroin. That is where the real money was. Wade had advised them to lay off Fentanyl (street names: Apache, TNT, China White, Goodfella and others). It was too dangerous, and resulted in many deaths around the country. It could bring serious heat. Opioids rounded off the best seller list. All in all, the cash kept pouring in. The boys prospered. The sudden death of Wade Brendon brought a dark cloud over their operation. They did not have a back-up supplier. They would need to scramble to fill the gap.

The day after Wade's murder the boys held a meeting at the house. David; "What the fuck are we going to do?

(73)

That freaking Wade. He must have double crossed his people on the supply line. We don't have any connection to the pipeline. We sure as hell, have got to find a new source."

Frank; "Davy boy, did you ever stop to think, that the supplier bumped off Wade. If so, what does that mean to us?"

"What do you mean by that?"

"Supposing, the supplier was somehow ripped off by Wade. The assholes might put two and two together, and come up with five. They might think we were involved with whatever scheme they tagged Wade for."

David; "That's something to consider. We've got to find a way to make contact with the bastards. The question is how?"

Morgan; "What if it wasn't the supplier? What if it was some other bastard that killed Wade? That might be just as bad. The supplier isn't going to like losing their distributor. They might still put us in their crosshairs with that line of thinking. They might conclude that, we had a falling out with Wade. The whole thing gives me the creeps. We'll be needing to keep looking over our shoulders."

The brothers wrestled with their dilemma the next couple of days. Those worries were brought to a secondary concern as they were raided by DEA. As is their want; the DEA team busted in on them in the middle of the night. It was a hella of an awaking. Three in the morning. They did not knock. Well, in fact, they did knock. But it was not a knock to plead for entry. It was a bombastic knock by a metal, door busting ramrod, followed by rushing boots. The house was suddenly filled with heavily armed agents.

The Ferrell brothers were taken into custody by DEA and Eugene Police task force. They were hauled into the County jail, or more literally, Lane County Adult Corrections Facility on Fifth Ave. Unfortunately for the brothers, they had been arrested, under a warrant, that also included a provision for search of the premises. Also, unfortunately for them, evidence had been discovered in the ensuing search. The evidence included various illegal substances including a kilo of heroin, and two kilos of coke. It was a total bust for the Ferrell's. They looked to be facing serious time. There was also the murder of Wade Brendon, their known supplier. They would automatically, be persons of interest in that case. The Feds passed the case on to the County D.A. for prosecution. The DEA would be credited for the bust along with the Eugene Police Task Force. Eugene Police Department would give commendation to Sgt. Allen Prebilsky, for his leadership part in the task force operation. This opened the door for Brad and Matt to interview the suspects.

Friday morning, the two Eugene Police detectives met with the detainees at county holding. It was an interrogation room, that both Brad and Matt were familiar with. They had held many interviews in the same room. A recording device was set in the middle of the table. The three men were brought in with handcuffs, but without shackles. They were seated side by side on one side of the table. Brad and Matt sat on the opposite side. Sitting at the end of the table, was an attorney, hired hurriedly by the brothers. Damon Jensen, attorney at law, had taken the case to defend the young men. It was important to the police, that the suspects had legal counsel. It is a matter of tidiness for the law, to be sure arrestees received due process.

Matt read to the recorder, the names of all present, and date and time of interview. Brad started out with questions.

"You are aware of the murder of Wade Brendon, are you not?"

The attorney nodded to Steve. Steve answered, "Yes. We have heard it on the news."

"Did you have any relations with the man. Did you have any business transactions with him?"

This time the attorney interceded. "Before we go into that, you need to explain, under what guise these questions are framed. Are my clients being subjected to this interview for reasons unrelated to their arrest warrant?"

Brad; "A man has been murder in his driveway. We have information that he was a supplier to your clients, of material, that is pertinent to their arrest. The drug pedaling charges are set in stone. My interest at this point is their potential involvement with the decedent, who once again; we have knowledge of their association with Brendon. We are only looking to see, if they had any beef with the man."

Damon; "Obviously that is a question out of bounds. My clients are not ready to plead guilty, or make any confession of guilt, in the matters contained in the arrest warrant. They are not, therefore, ready to admit to any involvement with your decedent. You may want to rephrase your question as to whether or not, they had any beef with the decedent."

"I see. Well gentlemen, I will ask, did you have any beef with Wade Brendon?"

Steve; "No."

Brad could see, that this interview was going nowhere. There was no way to force or maneuver around the stumbling block. He was fairly certain, that they were most likely to be convicted on the drug charges. His investigation of the murder case would be stalled on their account, unless he could find some evidence to give probable cause for a new warrant. There are times when, time becomes a huge factor in pursuing an investigation. The brothers would be due in court the following morning for their initial appearance.

"One last question Do you know of anybody that might have had a grudge with Brendon?"

That last question garnered a quick no and the interview was abated.

The recording device was disabled for the convenience of the attorney to consult in private with his clients.

Damon began talking to the brothers. "You boys have gotten yourself in a bear trap. Whatever possessed you to have such a large number of drugs at the house? This rises well above mere possession. The DA is going to push for trafficking. That means you do not get to walk automatically. There will be arguments for security release. That might take a few days. You know, these charges could mean a sentence of potentially twenty-five years. Not to mention, $375,000 in fines."

David; "We can cover the fine. But no way, on the long prison term."

"Well I'm certainly glad that the money is not a problem. The only way I can get you off, is to try to

(77)

suppress the search warrant. I have read the warrant, and I must say, it looks pretty tight. The only other defense I can think of, is to simply plead out. The strategy would be, to plead guilty to a lower charge. You have one thing in your favor. You have never been charged with drugs before.

"That's the best you can do for us?"

Damon; "It's the cards you've dealt me. All I can do, is try. You are not exactly clean, but no drug offenses in your record.

I'm afraid, you will be faced with some time behind bars. The question is how much or how little. I'll have to bluff my way through this. The question is, can I get it down to one or two years, providing I can make a deal?"

David; "It depends on how much time they will settle for. For our part two years is the max. But first, see if you can punch any holes in that warrant."

"I will take a hard look at it. Probable cause is the only part I can possibly challenge. The warrant was based on testimony, made by a couple of people, you have been dealing with. There are also surveillance photos, showing Brendon entering the house with a tote bag on numerous occasions. The police have taken custody of a bag from Brendon's residence, that resembles the one in the photos."

"Can you talk with the supposed witnesses? Maybe get them to change their story?"

"I have legal authority to interview the witnesses, yes. However, it is very tricky. There can be no indication of attempting to sway them. It's a matter of determining how positive they are, in the information they are giving to the authorities.

(78)

Chapter 14   Building a Case

The District attorney's office released a news release regarding the Brendon murder and the tie in to the Struthers murder. The DA gave the information of evidence, found on Brendon's camera, of Alexis Struthers taken at the crime scene, shortly after her death. The report went on, to make the conclusive findings, that Brendon was in fact, the murderer of Struthers, and that closed the files on the case. The murder of Brendon was an ongoing investigation. It was not ascertained at this time, whether or not the two murders were connected.

Friday morning, four days following Brendon's death, Brad and Matt were in their office at police headquarters. They were checking their notes and expounding on possible suspects in the Brendon murder.

Brad; "There are a few different ways to look at this case. One, we can take it for granted, that Brendon murdered Alexis. The photo in his personal camera pretty much sets that in concrete. He had plenty of motive and access. This brings us to his death. There are more than two ways to look at it. It may have been a revenge killing. That would put Robert on our list. Or it could have been a drug argument which puts the Ferrell brothers on the list. It could also be his supplier from out of state, that had a falling out with him. We need to find out who the supplier is, and where they are located. Hopefully DEA can help on that account."

Matt; "I almost hate to throw this in the pot. But what about Karen Morgan? She was deathly afraid of the man. She was emotionally distraught about being forced to lie to us. Maybe, she snapped, and did him in her own driveway. We haven't done a thorough search for a weapon on her premises.

Brad; "That's a long shot in my book. However, you could take that line of thinking a bit further. For instance, what if she was the killer in both cases. She could have motive for both killings. She may have been insanely jealous of Alexis. She had access to her boyfriend's camera. She could have done Alexis, taken the photo on Brendon's camera, with the idea of framing him for the job. Then, by shooting Wade in the driveway, put an end to the entire affair. However, I don't like that scenario at all. She would have to be one hell of an actress to pull it off. You've seen her. She comes off as clean as Snow-white. I can't believe, that she has the capacity for anything as wild as that."

Matt; "I'm with you on that. But, you yourself, have said, that looks can be deceiving. Sometimes you've got to put that aside and go with the facts and probabilities."

Brad; "Well, we won't write her off completely. Best thing to do is interview her again. Thoroughly as possible. See if there are any cracks. The oldest trick in the game can be co-operation. We should be on guard for anyone that is of interest and shows complete co-operation. It could smack of attempting to throw us off their trail. This would also apply to Robert. He has been extra co-operative. We'll have more talks with him as well. You go after Karen. I'll take Robert. See if we can arrange for interviews this afternoon."

Karen and Robert were each summoned by the police via telephone to come into the station for interviews. They both showed up at the police building at two in the afternoon. Matt was just returning from lunch. He was in the parking lot when Robert drove up in a sandstone colored Toyota. He greeted Robert in the lot, and walked into the building with him. Karen was not far behind them. Brad was in his office when Matt and Robert walked in. They had just gotten seated when the desk clerk buzzed, that Karen Morgan was here for her interview.

"Matt, you can see Karen. Take her in the interrogation room. I'll chat with Robert."

"Will do." Matt wrote a quick not and slid it over to Brad. It read; 'Robert/sand colored Toyota rental.'

"Robert, do you feel comfortable talking to me without your attorney?"

"I think so. If you ask me something scary, I may have to defer. As I have previously stated, I do not have anything to hide."

"You understand, the murder of Alexis is a closed file. It remains however, as a potential link to the murder of Wade Brendon. It is possible, it was an act of revenge taken upon Wade. That puts you back on the list of persons of interest. I have to consider, that you might have had great feeling of hate for Wade. Considering that he stole from you, your dreams of the future. Do you care to respond to that?"

"First of all, I am a computer scientist. I deal with numbers and facts. I had no way to determine for sure, that Wade had killed Alexis. All I knew, was that he might be a person of interest. The factual knowledge or evidence, that points to him as being the factual killer, was not known to me until yesterday, when the District Attorney released the news concerning the photographs on Wade's personal camera. I can tell you, that even with that Knowledge, I would not have taken criminal action

(81)

against the man. Maybe, that puts a dent in my shining armor. But I am not a violent person. I would have left it to the law. I believe in justice, not vigilantism."

"You have rented a sand colored Toyota, is that correct?"

"Yes. I didn't feel comfortable driving Alee's car. I needed wheels, seeing as how, I am remaining in town, at least until after tomorrow's services. I can at least rest assured, that her killing has been solved. I am only sorry, that the killer is, in a way, off the hook. I mean, it would have been much better, had he stood trial for his evil deed."

"I'm afraid there a few points that we will have to sort out. One, is that you were deeply in love with Alexis. She was murdered by her ex-boyfriend. You certainly had strong reason to believe he was guilty. Two, you are driving a sand colored auto. We have a witness that claims to have seen a like automobile, driving down the street immediately after the shooting of Wade. Three, you cannot substantiate your whereabouts at the time of the shooting. This adds up to the facts, that you had motive, accessibility, and a car that fits the description of the car on the street. Do you own a .38 caliber pistol?"

"No. I do not. Now, I am getting a bit worried. You seem to be aiming a guilty banner at me. I don't think, I had better answer anything else until I bring in my attorney. I did want to co-operate as much as possible."

"I'm trying my best to eliminate you as a person of interest. I need to work through your profile and discard everything that keeps you in the picture. But, I do not blame you for wanting your attorney present. Are you planning on leaving town?"

(82)

"Yes. Sometime after the funeral tomorrow for Alexis. Will that pose any problem?"

"No. You are free to go. Just be sure, that we can contact you without any hassle. Remember, you are not a suspect in Brendon's murder. I just need to make sure there are no stones left unturned. You are free to leave."

After Robert left his office, Brad decided to run a data base check on the man. He had his address in San Jose. He started with that to verify the address. It came up positive. There were no criminal records. Not even a parking violation. He ran the name through California's gun registration data. It made a hit. A Smith and Wesson .38 special caliber revolver four years ago. The serial number and purchase point were there on the screen. Brad almost bit his lip. 'The son of a bitch lied.' He pondered the discovery for a few moments. A lie like this, could only mean cover-up. The man was trying to conceal something. Was his older brother somehow involved? Did he go out and commit the act of revenge on his own? Is he mentally unstable?

Brad had only one choice. He would gather up all his notes and files on the case and visit the DA. He made the call to the county DA's office and asked Deputy DA Oliver Stoltz for a meeting.

Matt came into the office and with a wave of his hand, "There's nothing new, I could get out of her. She is sticking with her original story, right down the line."

Brad went over his interview with Robert. "The asshole lied to me about something extremely material. I asked if he owned a .38 handgun. He answered without batting an eye, that he did not."

(83)

"Well, that certainly casts a new shadow on his co-operation mode. What are you going to do?"

"What can I do? I'm going over to the DA's office and lay it out for them. Let them make the call, as to whether or not we have probable cause."

"I'll join you."

The two detectives drove over to the county prosecutor's office and was met by Oliver Stoltz. Stoltz was a Deputy Agent for the DA. He tried many of the high-profile cases that came through the door. He had been with the DA for nine years. He had a solid reputation for trying hard-nosed cases.

"What have you got for me, Brad?"

Brad went over the Brendon murder case with Oliver. He recalled the interview he had just completed with a person of interest, Robert Barclay. He told of the lie that Barclay had bombed on him regarding the pistol. That information along with the matching car at the scene, and his motive potential, might be enough to elevate the man from person of interest to a suspect for murder.

Oliver studied the notes. He sat back in his chair with folded hands behind his head. He swiveled towards Matt. "What is your take Matt?"

"I've been with Brad throughout this investigation. I was not present, when he did the interview this afternoon. He doesn't seem like the type. But in our business, that is sometimes, just who is the type. We need to be concerned, that our prospect is from out of state. He lives in San Jose, California. Most likely, he will be headed home after the services for his sweetheart tomorrow. The question, then becomes, whether or not, he decides to go jackrabbit. He could skip. I think that's why we are here for this quick meet. Do we haul him in, or wait it out?"

Brad; "That's about the size of it. You need to make the call."

"We have enough here to satisfy Judge Holgarth for a warrant based on probable cause." The judge was known to be friendly with the law enforcement agencies, and easy on the probable cause requirements. "What do we lose if we are wrong? I would like a little bit more, to take to a grand jury. I'll ask for the warrant. But you boys have got to work overtime, and dig up what you can between now and Tuesday. I can work a delay on the first appearance until then. Are you still looking at the drug connection with the Ferrell's? Or have you already scrubbed them?"

Brad; "No. We are still digging for them as well. However, we have them under wraps over at county on drug trafficking. We should be able to keep them on ice while we dig."

"Good enough. It may be material in my work on that case. I am sure I'll be hearing from their attorney, Damon Jensen, on a cop out offer. We have them dead to rights on trafficking. Okay. I'll secure the warrant on Barclay. I suggest you make the pickup at graveside tomorrow."

Brad drove out to Memorial Gardens Saturday noon. The mortuary services had been held for Alexis Struthers. The procession had made its way to the cemetery. There was a brief ceremony at the grave site. The crowd was beginning to disperse. Robert was walking towards his car with the parents. Brad intercepted the trio and said they would like to speak to Robert in private. A courtesy as it were. They could have arrested and cuffed him right there in front of everybody.

(85)

"Of course, officer. What can I do for you?"

After Brad explained the situation to Robert, Robert turned to the Struthers and said he would need to go to police headquarters for further interviews with the detectives. He handed Edward the Toyota car keys, and asked if it would be okay to keep the car at their house until he got squared away.

Edward; "No problem Bob. It'll be in the driveway until you pick it up."

Brad and Robert were in Brad's car, headed towards the Eugene Police Station. Brad had decided to do the booking there, and hold Robert in the station holding cell. It would be less public, since it was unoccupied at the time. He felt it might go a bit easier with Robert. He wasn't entirely sure, that the arrest was the right move. It was all a matter of circumstance. If only Robert had not lied about the gun.

In the car, Robert; "It seems, I have graduated from person of interest to suspect rather quickly. Is there some revelation, I should be aware of?"

Brad; "It's a combination of evidence and circumstances. The hard blow is, you lied to me about not owning a certain gun."

Robert mused over that statement for a moment. "Brad, you asked me if I owned a .38 caliber handgun. The answer to that is still no. I do not."

"Damn it Robert. We ran a check on gun registration in California. Four years ago, you purchased a Smith and Wesson .38 special revolver. The records do not lie. There is no record of you transferring the gun to another person. Do you still deny that?"

"I can certainly explain it. The truth is, I bought the gun for my company. I was reimbursed for it. The gun was used in an experiment. It was a complicated experiment. The idea was to create a new type of aiming device. It became unpractical and led to another project. A much bigger project. That is all I can tell you about the project, other than it is highly sensitive and wrapped as 'top secret.' This classification is not merely self-imposed, but is also classified as such by the government. I cannot say any more than that. As far as the gun is concerned, it is the property of Digital Autonomous Intelligent Programs. That is where I work."

"Okay. We'll check it out. If that's the truth, it will go much better for you. Why didn't you tell me all that, when I asked about the gun?"

"like I said. I did not own any such gun. Yes, I purchased one a few years ago, but I never truly had possession of it."

Once booked at the police department detention center, with photos, and prints taken, Robert was allowed to call his attorney and brother in California. His first call was to William Jacobs, attorney. He told of his arrest and incarceration. William replied that he would come to the station house and meet with him. "Try not to say much until I get there."

The second call was to his brother Steve. "Stevie, I'm in a snare. The cops have arrested me as a suspect in the Wade Brendon murder. I might have made a slight goof, when I was asked If I owned a .38 caliber handgun. My answer was no. Now they think I lied, after running a registration check in California. They came across that gun, I bought for the company project four years ago. I have no idea, what the company did with the gun. The project I bought it for, went south for various reasons, that I am

(87)

sure, you are aware of. I have called Jacobs. He is on his way here now. I'm sorry for the screw up."

Steve; "Not to worry. We both know you are innocent. I'll fly up tomorrow. Just keep calm, and watch what you say."

After hanging up, Steve made a call to the National Security Agent that acted as liaison on the Centurion project. This was a project that DAIP had proposed to the pentagon. It had drawn great interest by the military. It was a project that was based on developing a 100% accurate missile defense system. It held great promise and was classified top secret. All DAIP employees were forced to go through background checks, and extensive interviews with the FBI. Once vetted, they were given security clearance to work on the project. The facilities that housed all labs and workshops for the project, were guarded by military police. Robert had been vetted, and had clearance to work on the project. This had been of tantamount importance to the project, as it was Robert, that had developed the concept, and would be the lead technician on its progression. All vetted employees were assigned clearance badges necessary for entrance to the facilities. No outsiders were allowed in, without cleared chaperones, and written permission from CIA, FBI, or NSA. It was a highly protected enterprise. The military considered it a world changer, if completed and proven successful. Robert was absolutely assured it would meet the tests. He projected the final prototype to be on line in eighteen months.

For the time being he was housed in a cell in the Eugene Police Department station. He had been told that his initial court appearance would be Tuesday morning.

(88)

Monday morning early, Brad got a call from the chief District Attorney, Pamela Menninger. She needed his immediate attendance in her office. In his official business routines, her's was a voice to be harkened to. "I'll be there in ten."

Brad delivered as promised and entered the DA's office at eight-twenty AM. There were two suits in her office as he entered. Pamela greeted Brad and asked him to sit at the conference table in the corner of the room alongside the two suits. One suit belonged to CIA and the other to NSA. A fact that Brad was soon to be apprised of. "Brad this is Toby Marlow from NSA, and Chase Vinson from CIA."

"Happy to meet you gentleman." Looking straight in the eyes of Chase Vinson, "I never met a CIA agent before. This is a first. You guys stay pretty much in the background."

"Oh shit. You just broke my cover." This Chase said with a stern disgruntled look across the agent's face. Serious as hell.

Brad was dumbfounded. Was this guy for real? A few seconds passed, then, Chase let out a low-pitched chuckle "You should see the look on your face."

Brad opined that the agency must have some humor. Weird as it may be. Or perhaps this was just your typical gagster, who happened to end up in the agency. He figured it was not a material factor to prejudge the man. Could very well be, that he was a top-notch agent. Besides that, a little humor never hurt anyone. And in this case, Brad got the joke. He played along. "I didn't know you were working undercover. My bad." He snorted a short laugh.

(89)

Pamela; "Brad, these men are here, in regards to your recent arrest, of one Robert Barclay on suspicion of homicide. It seems they have an interest in the man."

Chase; "This is the situation. You are holding a key man, in a military project of national interest. He is the most important man on the project. I cannot tell you the nature of the project, other than what I have just stated. This of course, does not mean, that we have any intention in interfering in your murder investigation. It is important however, that we are made privy to all statements the man has made to you, or any other authority. You might call it potential damage control, concerning top secret information. We need to know exactly what conversations and disclosures; the suspect might have made to you. Particularly, anything regarding his vocation and work. And especially any projects."

Brad; "I see. I can tell you that he has not been questioned about his work. We detained him primarily because, I thought, I had caught him in a lie about a particular gun. I assume you are up-to date on the case he is tied to."

"We would look rather foolish were we not. Intelligence is our bread and butter. We have studied very close, the entire matter, including background checks on all officers involved in the case. That of course includes yourself. The main question is how strong is your intention, to pursue a conviction against our subject. The evidence we have studied, seems quite thin and circumstantial. We have done a research on the revolver in question. There is no doubt, that the gun is in the custody of DAIP."

Pamela; "Brad, it is my opinion that with the revelation of the gun being taken into account, the

(90)

warrant is somewhat flawed. I will have to drop the charges for now. You may keep Mr. Barclay on your list of persons of interest. The case is still wide open. You will need to co-operate with these gentlemen as to any security breach. Please make all your notes involving the suspect available to them. The prisoner will be released immediately."

Brad; "I understand. I will be happy to work with the government. I assume you will be taking him back to San Jose?" Brad directed the question to the two Feds.

Chase; "The sooner, the better. He has important work to do, as do I. It is imperative that no loose information has been compromised regarding the project. If you have your files with you, perhaps we can go over them here and now."

Brad; "I have all my files and notes on the case here in my briefcase. I came prepared. Not exactly for this. But all the same, here they are." Brad dug out the various folders from his briefcase, and laid them on the table. He pushed them over to Chase. Chase and Tobey began looking through the files, and handwritten notes.

Pamela's secretary buzzed her to say, that William Jacobs would like some time with her. Pamela replied that she would step out and meet William in the foyer. She met the attorney outside her office and walked with him into a conference room. Once inside; "I know what's on your mind. You need not go into it just now. Your man is being released this morning. The homicide charge has been dropped for now. He remains a person of interest in the case. Please advise him, that under no circumstances should he attempt to leave the country."

William agreed. He asked if there was new information he could share. Pamela related, that new

(91)

evidence indicated, that Robert's supposed lie about owning a certain type of gun had proven to be a mistaken communication. The bureau was satisfied that he was telling the truth.

"Well, that is certainly good news. I'll be sure to admonish him to stay in the country."

"Thanks for stopping by. I have people in my office, and I need to get right back in there."

The two federal agents before adjourning the meeting with the DA and Brad, insisted that their being in Eugene, not be disclosed to the media or public. "The less people, that know we were here, the better."

Tobey and Chase departed the office and drove to the police station where Robert was being detained. The call desk had already been advised by the DA's office to release Robert Barclay. When the two Federal agents arrived at the station, Robert was already being processed for release. They sidled up to him and Chase whispered in his ear, that he would need to travel with them back to San Jose. They had a six-passenger government jet waiting on the Eugene airport tarmac.

As they left the station, and were getting in to the Fed's rental car, Robert said he would need to check out of…. "The Hilton", Chase finished the sentence. "We'll get you checked out of the hotel and be on our way.

"I have a rental parked at the Struthers. I need to pick it up and check it in."

"Not to worry. We have you covered. Someone will take care of the car for you. We need to be airborne as soon as possible. We will be debriefing you on the aircraft."

(92)

Robert worried about the effect all this might be having on Mom and Pop. He asked Chase if it would be okay to call them and explain.

"Sure, go ahead. But try to keep it brief. And not too much on the explanation end."

Robert called and got Edward on the phone. He explained that he had been called back to San Jose on a business emergency, and that the company would have someone pick up the Toyota and check it in for him. He told them not to worry, everything was fine. And that he had finalized his meeting with the police satisfactorily.

Chase had called the pilot waiting at the airport and told him to be ready to lift off in ten minutes. Both pilots worked for the agency and had top secret clearance. Upon arriving at the airport, the men grabbed their luggage from the trunk and left the keys in the car, in spot twelve of the Hertz return parking lot. From there they proceeded through the gate next to Friendly Air Service. Not far from that gate, the agency jet sat ready for action. The door was open, and the three men hustled into the cabin of the aircraft.

After liftoff and airborne, Chase began questioning Robert about his treatment by the police. He wanted as much verbatim of his talks to the police as possible. Robert concentrated hard and gave what he could of all the interviews with the police. He told of mentioning DAIP to Brad in regards to the pistol that had aroused so much concern. "I never mentioned anything about our projects."

"That's good. We will monitor the situation. We will see if anything comes out in the media. I think we are probably good to go. You are sure you didn't mention anything to anybody else?"

(93)

"Dead sure."

One hour and ten minutes after liftoff, the jet landed at the San Jose airport. Robert had left his car in long term parking. The agents bid him goodbye and remained on the jet, ready to depart back to Virginia. "If you get any more flak, be sure to call this number." As Chase handed him his personal card. "Stay out of trouble, and be careful about pickups in a bar." He grinned broadly upon making the parting remark.

Chapter 15   Appliances and Other Goods

Jesse Rodriquez had heard the news of the murder of Wade Brendon on the news. Portland is ninety-five miles north of Eugene on Interstate 5. Portland is the metro city in the state. It is surrounded by several bedroom communities, some of which are hard to define as being separated from Portland proper. Portland's city population is 630,000. The metro, area consisting of seven counties, is home to just over half of the state's population of four million two hundred thousand people. The metro area population as of 2017 stands at 2,150,000.

Jesse was the distributor, in the Portland metro area, for Manuel Contreras of San Diego. The merchandise was illegal or controlled substance. High on the menu of goods was heroin. Second would be cocaine. From there on down was a sundry list of Meth, opioids, and a variety of street drugs. He was in fact, the counterpart to Wade Brendon in the smaller community of Eugene, with a metro area population of 370,000. Jesse had called Manuel to pass on information of the Murder of Wade Brendon. It was Tuesday morning, just three days after the killing.

Manuel; "Son of a bitch. That crazy fucking gringo. Who did him? Did he try to fuck over somebody? He was always square with me. Maybe he tried a short count on one of his customers. It would have to be the Ferrell boys. They were his biggest drop. Do you hear anything on the streets up there in Portland?"

"No Manny. I picked it up on the regular news. The papers say, he has been identified as a man, who killed his ex-girlfriend, just a few days earlier. The police are looking at a possible revenge killing. Are you going to need me to fill in down there in Eugene? And I am sure you heard about the Ferrell brothers

bust. The DEA took them down in the middle of the night. They're in county jail as we speak. They were caught holding."

"Fuck. That tears it. Those boys were my main pushers. Or I should say, Wade's main clients. He didn't think, I knew who his drops were. But you can bet your ass, I knew all along. You think, I'm gonna fly in the dark and not know who's handling my merchandise on the street. Look, I'm gonna need you, to step up. I need you to set up a crew in Eugene. You should be able to handle it with a couple of good people. You're doing a good job in Portland. Eugene is much smaller. You shouldn't have any problem working things out. It shouldn't be too hard to flesh out the brother's street vendors. What do you say?"

"I can do it. No problem. The only thing is, the boys might get free. They might be ready to resume business as usual. They haven't been indicted yet."

"No fuck that. As far as I'm concerned, they are toast. If they were caught red handed with stuff at the house, they are going up. And, if by some miracle they are set loose, no matter. They're finished with me. Too much risk. Too much exposure." Manuel felt confident that he had little to worry about over the brother's arrest. He knew who they were, but they had no knowledge about his involvement. That is, so long as Wade played it smart. Wade was a typical thug. But he had Moxy. He would never disclose his source to anyone. That would be a liability. Why let anyone know where the flow was coming from? He would be cutting his own throat. Potentially cutting himself out of the picture. No, he would have kept

(96)

that information under his vest. It all works to Manuel's interest. 'Good, that the little people keep things to themselves. In the end, it helps keeping that wall around me. Funny thing
about secrets. One person, might keep safe guarded a dozen secrets. A dozen people, cannot keep safe, one shared secret. The very proof of that, is shown daily by government leaks. Too many ears. Too many personal agendas, that feed on being able to spread the word. Too many egos looking for the limelight. Those bastards will go to any length, for putting themselves in the spotlight. Even if it means inventing gossip. It all ends up in the fake news media.'

Jesse; "Right boss. I will get right on it. I can spare the time. Things are cool here on this end. I've got good people to fill in for me. Keep the Portland deliveries as before. You might add a couple of kilos in the next shipment. We'll need stock for down south."

"You're a good hombre Jesse. I knew I could count on you. Keep me posted on the brothers."

Manuel Contreras had built a lucrative and well protected assembly and distribution of narcotics. He ran a legitimate appliance business in San Diego. He purposely did not distribute in his own backyard. He kept his dealings strictly as a whole seller. He had zero distribution in the San Diego metro area. All of his merchandise was shipped out of the area. The people who did the running to the various markets north and east, were handled by a third party. They had no direct connection to Manuel. They could only guess where the shipments were originated. The man, that managed the shipment dispatches, was totally trusted by Manuel. The setup gave Manuel a solid wall of insulation from prying eyes. The only people that knew of his involvement where the distributors at the other end. Brendon was the only one, he had any doubts about. His sudden death might have been a blessing. He was no longer a person to be concerned about. Jesse on the other hand, had his full confidence right down the line. Wade would be the last non-Latino to be entrusted as a distributor.

Not to bemoan the loss of Wade, Manuel decided to send a team up to Eugene to investigate his death. He had admonished Jesse, to keep him posted on any news regarding Wade' death. However, his concern was whether or not, the death was in any way connected to any local rivalry, or outside forces looking to take over the market. This required a close look. Having a competitor move on his setup was anathema. Especially when violence was part of the plot. This is a business, that must fight fire with fire. Being muscled out of a market could become a death spiral. He had selected markets in six states. It was a momentous task that took several years to build. He could little afford to give up any hard-gained territory.

Manuel would have a crew from Salinas gather, and make plans to travel to Eugene. These were his elite forces. Hard men. Men, that could hold their own in any tough situation. Street wise men. But more than anything else, they were men totally loyal to Manuel. They were not vendors on the street. They were more akin, to being his secret police. It was their duty to keep people in line. It was their job to handle all disputes. In some cases, it was their job to execute offenders. The leader of this select group was Antonio DeLeon.

Manuel had no feeling of conscious regarding his nefarious goods, being peddled on the streets across the west and northwest. The rising number of heroin overdose deaths didn't sway his feelings. He opined it was a matter of supply and demand. His only role was to supply. He had no design on demand. He was only supplying what people wanted or needed. If he didn't supply it, someone else surely would.

Chapter 16   Running low on Suspects

Two weeks after the murder of Wade Brendon, Brad and Matt were still working the case. The Ferrell Brothers had been found guilty vis a vis plea bargaining, of trafficking in illegal substance. The DA had negotiated with their attorney and settled on six years and $380,000 penalty. The felony record would follow them the rest of their lives. Part of the plea arraignment was that they would co-operate with the local police regarding the murder investigation of Brendon. A second part, was that they would co-operate with DEA regarding any connections they might have with narcotic suppliers.

Brad and Matt interviewed the brothers at county as they were waiting transfer to the state prison system. It became evident that they had nothing to do with the murder. It also became clear, that they had little knowledge about major drug suppliers. All they knew, was that Brendon was their source.

Brad greatly feared, that the case on Brendon might go cold. There were no leads to chew on. Robert Barclay was the best he had, but there was no real evidence against him. The sandstone color of his rental car was purely circumstantial. Even that evidence was weak. Not enough description to rely on. He didn't seem to fit the profile of a killer. Of course, not all killers fit the profile. If they did, murder cases would be all the easier to track and solve. Too many times, it was that nice young man next door. Sometimes, a murder is completely irrational. That is, there may not be any motive. This is not true of serial or mass murders. They do have motive. A motive of self-aggrandizement. A motive to satisfy a blood lust.

Usually social misfits that have strong urgency to strike out at society. In a word, unbalanced. Could the Brendon murder be one such?

"Brad, I'm thinking this thing is looking more and more like some kind of drug thing. We know Brendon was a major supplier for the local vendors. One scenario, could be a hit by some disgruntled pusher. I know we have weeded out his main buyers, but there could be some small fry out there, that had a grudge to settle with him. Or two, some out of town competitor getting rid of the competition. Maybe, some new players muscling the market."

"I really don't know Matt. Prebilsky is working with DEA. I haven't heard any report on any activity that would suggest any new players. But, I like your idea about the small fry. This might be a good time to set up a task force to reign in street pushers. Interrogating the low life might spring a lead. I'll check it out with the chief."

Brad presented the idea to Chief of Police. Michael Kerry.

"Well Brad. I don't see any problem on setting up a task force for that. Hell, it will be good policy even without the Brendon affair. The public loves crackdowns. Drugs or prostitution. Take your pick. Either one makes good headlines. Should you pick up any leads on your case, all the better. There is one glitch. You need to check with Sergeant Prebilsky. Make sure your force will not run up against any operation, DEA may have ongoing."

"I'm ahead of you on that chief. I wouldn't think of moving without checking with Al."

The meeting with Sergeant Prebilsky made a dent in Brad's plan to form a task force. DEA had been doing an intensive investigation on the movement of heroin in the area.

"Brad, we think drugs are moving in the area again. It looks to be coming from Portland. Our hunch is, it is the same outfit. We suspect the main supplier has a network covering the entire northwest. It is very likely that the drugs coming in, are from the same supplier. We have a couple of agents working undercover on the streets, as you and I sat here. We have tips from some of the vendors on the street. I can make sure you get access to anyone hauled in. The net is tightening."

"Sounds great, Al. I certainly would like to interview some of the low-life. I'm up against it on the Brendon case. A drug connection seems the most likely scenario."

"Yeah. Shoot-ups are not that uncommon amongst dealers and pushers. It could even possibly be a user. However, like I said, there's movement going on. It's like a vacuum. Make an opening, and surely something has to fill it. Way too much money involved. Shit, sometimes, I think why not legalize the whole caboodle. Take the profit out of it. Cut the gangster's cash flow. I do think, it would be less chaos, were it all available. You know. The same as weed. I tell you this Brad; because I don't think the battle will ever end. The way it stands, People are killing each other and yes, many people are dying from it. But for every bust we make, as I said, the vacuum only invites new players. In essence, it's a losing battle. The only winners are the bad guys. It's a fucking national epidemic."

"Well, look on the bright side. It keeps a lot of us good guys employed."

Chapter 17   Clueless

Antonio and his crew had been in Eugene for two full weeks. They had talked to several people on the street, including many homeless. They had offered cash for any information regarding Brendon. Antonio had met with Jesse to let him know of his mission in the area. Jesse swore to co-operate by sharing any information he came across. Jesse was well acquainted with Antonio's reputation as an enforcer for Manuel. He knew the man could be ruthless. He felt sorry for anybody that fell prey to his investigation. He was known to use inquisition style of interrogating. He was also known as the widow maker.

The search for information in Eugene had been fruitless. However, Antonio and Jesse could report that there was no evidence on interloping by outsiders. None of the street pushers in Eugene, were of a caliber, that could take advantage of Brendon's death. Brendon's killer was a total mystery. It had to be from outside the industry. Some personal grudge or other. Brendon was known to be a ladies' man. Perhaps, one of those ladies had an unwilling boyfriend or husband, that didn't shine to his amorous attentions to their stock. When Antonio reported to Manuel, he gave an all clear signal that no harm had been done to the organization. Brendon would need to be avenged by others. Police had not made any arrests in the case as of yet.

"Okay, Tony. Load up and head home. I might need to send you over to Phoenix next week. We seem to have lost a package of merchandise. Call me Monday."

Antonio finished up his work in Eugene and loaded up the van with his crew, and headed back to Salinas,

California. He hoped for more action in Phoenix. Tracking missing merchandise was his specialty. It usually involved final rites for some perpetrator.

Jesse had settled in in Eugene. It was a snap. It didn't take long to ferret out the pushers and vendors for the goods. He rented a small house in the Churchill area west of town. It was a middleclass neighborhood. Neatly trimmed houses and yards. This was an area for middle-class families. Quiet and peaceful. This would put him in an unassuming surrounding. Less attention from prying eyes and ears. He also rented a small office on Garfield Street. He would do all his transactions from there.

It was three weeks since Wade's murder. A ceremony had been announced. There had been delays, due to the autopsy and notification of next of kin. The only next of kin to be found, was Wade's mother. She had finally, been tracked down in her hometown of Steubenville, Ohio. Tracking her had been difficult, being that his mother had been remarried to Robert Whitehead many years ago, shortly after becoming a widow. Wade had retained his own father's last name, unlike Dino Paul Crocetti, born the son of a barber from that same town. It wasn't divorce of parents, that Dino changed his name. It was reaching for stardom in the entertainment world, that encouraged him to change his name to Dean Martin.

Wade's services were set for Saturday. His mother would be attending. Mr. Whitehead would not. Barbara Brendon Whitehead had been estranged from her son for many years. However, motherhood being what it is, she could not think of not saying final farewell to her only son. She was horrified at the thought, of her son having been so brutally murdered.

(104)

Brad would also be attending the ceremonies. Not so much as deference to the man, but rather as a further part of his ongoing investigation. It would be his intention, to survey any attendees that might ignite further queries.

There was but a small group at the services and the following internment at graveside. The sixteen by sixteen-foot canvas gazebo easily sheltered the group from the steady falling rain. Rain has a certain quality, solidifying the austere ritual for the departing soul. Brad was surprised to see the Struthers at the two ceremonies. After the ceremony at graveside, Brad sidled up to Alexis' parents. "Well, this would be the last chapter for Wade. I was surprised some, to see you here."

Edward; "Yes. I suppose this is the end for Wade in this world. I worry for his soul. Myrna and I pray for him. He has a lot to answer for when he meets God."

Brad; "Yes. I am sure he does. Do I take it, you have found in your heart to forgive him?"

"It is the province of the Lord to forgive. It is our province, to not let another's sins darken our heart. I admit, I had severe hateful feelings towards the man. However, I took the road, the Lord assigned me. I still have problems forgetting the dreadful harm he has done, but as far as judgement, I leave that up to Christ."

The crowd was beginning to disperse. Brad wanted to take this opportunity, to meet Wade's mother. He saw her standing next to the preacher, that had conducted the services. He said goodbye to the Struthers, and watched as they walked towards their car. He took a quick mental note of the car. It was a Ford Fusion. It was sandstone colored.

Brad approached the preacher and Mrs. Whitehead.

"That was a fine ceremony Reverend Gallagher. Very eloquent. It is a shame there weren't more folks here to participate. And you must be Wade's mother. I am Brad Ferguson. I work for the Eugene Police Department. My condolences for your loss. I didn't know your son well. I had met him only twice."

"Thank you for your care. I am Wade's mother; my name is Lana Whitehead. I was widowed when Wade was very young. I remarried a few years after Wade's father died in an auto accident. I know that Wade was in some trouble with the law. He has not communicated with me for decades. I guess you could say; we were not very close. I think, he resented my remarrying. It was after that, that he became different. More resentful and more troublesome to deal with. He left home at seventeen. It looks like, he ended up here. A long way from Steubenville."

Chapter 18   The Only Clue So Far

Monday, following Wade's services, Brad was in his office at headquarters. He sat with Matt and discussed the Brendon case. "I didn't learn much from the ceremony for Brendon. The only people there were his mother, the Struthers, and a couple of people from Merkle Reality. Karen didn't show. I can't say I blame her. About the only thing I learned was, that the Struthers drive a sandstone colored Ford Fusion."

"Ah so. What do you think that might be worth on the evidence scale?"

"I know it sounds crazy. But it does give us one small tie-in to the evidence we now have. That is, Karen's testimony, that she thought she saw a sandstone colored compact driving away from the scene. Then, there is the question of motive. Revenge is a powerful emotional game-changer. Admittingly, that doesn't seem to have much legs in this case. It would be hard to convince me, that the parents had anything to do with the demise of Brendon. But right at this moment, it is the only clue we have to work on. We will need to put it to bed, one way or another."

"So, we make a call on the Struthers?"

"I don't see any way around it."

Brad and Matt drove out to the Struthers residence. They had not called ahead. The strategy would be, to come unannounced, leaving the folks no time to ponder, what the reason for the call could possibly be. Once again, Edward answered the door. He must have had his early morning cigar. There was that tell-tell aroma emitting from his clothes.

(107)

"Officer, good morning. Please come in. What brings you here this morning?"

Brad; "I wanted to see how you and the missus were doing. I know you have been going through a lot this last few weeks. If there is anything, I can do for you, I am at your service."

Edward; "Oh, you need not bother. I do appreciate the thought. Myrna and I, have laid all our miseries before the Lord. It is in him, that we get our strength, and will to go on with life. Now tell me the truth. There must be something on your mind, that brings you here today."

"Ed, I need to go over a couple of items with you and your wife. It's just a matter of routine. In an investigation of homicide, we have to turn over every rock that might be holding information in our case. This part of our investigation, is mostly concerned about removing people from being a person of interest. You and your wife could be considered persons of interest in the Wade Brendon homicide. The facts, that make this so, are firstly; your relationship with the victim. The fact, that it was strongly believed at the time of his killing, that he was the suspected murderer of your daughter. Secondly; by coincidence, you happen to own a sandstone colored automobile. A witness at the murder scene testified, that she saw such a colored car driving away from the scene of the shooting."

"Yes, I see. I do own a sandstone colored car. That is a fact. I did suspect very strongly from the start, that Wade killed Alexis. That also is a fact. Hopefully, those two facts are not designating me as a killer. I mean, are you here to tell me, that I am now a suspect for murder?"

"Not at all. These two items are merely coincidences."

(108)

Edward: "Yet, you are here for some sort of clarification. Is that right? You must have many questions to ask of me."

"Ed, as I have said, the need as of now, is to clear you from any suspicions. It is important for us to do this. We have to take each step, one at a time. We follow the facts, wherever they lead us. The idea of investigators working on gut feelings and hunches, is somewhat a myth. It is really more like mathematics. We keeping gathering data, witness reports, sometimes forensics, and calculate a few things such as motive, access, and alibis. Then, it is a matter of adding it all up."

"In that case, I must ask, what is it you expect from me, other than what I have already admitted to?"

"Let's start with alibi. Can you, account for your whereabouts on Saturday morning of the shooting?"

Matt was taking notes of the conversation as Ed answered "Yes I can. Myrna and I were here at the house all morning that day."

"Ed, do you own any type of firearm? Most especially, do you own a .38 caliber pistol?" The police had reckoned the weapon to be a revolver as opposed to an automatic type handgun. This was deduced, by the lack of any cartridge casings found at the scene. A revolver does not eject spent casings. They stay in the chamber until manually ejected. An automatic type hand gun spits the used casings several feet away from the firing gun. In the Brenden killing, the shooter would not have had time to gather up any spent casings.

"I used to. I don't recall what ever happened to it. It's been years since I have seen it."

For Brad, this added yet another leg to the circumstances involving Edward Struthers, as a person of interest. Not quite enough to propel him into the arena of suspects. But he was hovering dangerously close to the perimeter. "Ed, this is very important. You need to obtain an attorney to represent you. I have to accept the fact, that you are a person of interest. This means, that we will have to do an intensive investigation of you and your wife. You should see an attorney right away. I may be forced to bring you in to the police station, for more interviews. Interviews that would be recorded and used in any proceedings. It is tantamount important, that you find the gun in question, so we can check ballistics against the ammo fired into Wade. This would enable us to discount your gun as the one used in the homicide, if the bullets do not match. It's a very scientific and reliable way of matching ammo fired from a gun against the bullets taken out of the victim. So, do your best to locate your revolver and let us check it out."

"Yes. That sounds like a good idea. I'll search for it. It must be here somewhere."

Brad and Matt were on their way back downtown.

Matt; "What are you thinking? Is there something going on with Ed?"

"I'm not sure. I'm not sure about anything. Ed is the last person I would suspect. He had motive for sure. But it seems to go against the grain of the man. He's a man of faith. It would be against his beliefs to do such a thing. Let's hope he comes up with his gun, and it clears ballistics."

"Everything you say is true. You know, that still leaves Myrna. She had as much motive as her husband. She could have pulled the trigger. It could even be a case of their working it together."

(110)

Chapter 19   The Arrest

Two days after the visit from the detectives, Edward Struthers called for an attorney. After a few references, he ended up with Leland Costello. Leland was a criminal defense attorney with twenty-two years of court practice. He had been referred by another firm, as being the best in the field. Leland offered Edward to come to his office and talk things over. This would be a no charge consultation. If Ed was satisfied with him, and Leland was of the persuasion to take the case, his rates would be $375 an hour and $600 an hour for court attendance. Any need for investigative work to be done any contractor, would be discussed first and approved by Edward. Leland liked to make clear to any new client, his fees and possible outside costs, should they arise. Best to have that settled at the start.

In his office on Park Street, downtown Eugene, He invited Edward and Myrna into his conference room. "So, let's start from the beginning. You have some mix-up with the local police?"

Edward; "You might say that. What has happened, is our daughter was murdered by this man named Wade Brendon. Shortly after her death, Brendon was also murdered. He was shot down with a handgun. The police seem to think it was a .38 caliber pistol. I have owned such a gun. But I haven't laid eyes on it for years. I'm trying to locate it, so it can be tested by the police. The police think, I might be of interest, for the sake of revenge for my daughter. And, I have admitted to owning a gun as they have described. They also have a witness, saying they saw a car colored the same as my Ford, driving away from the shooting. Right now, they are only saying Myrna and I are persons of interest in their investigation. They warned, that we may be called in for more interviews. They say, they will be investigating us thoroughly."

"I see. I am somewhat aware of the case of Brendon. I am also aware, through news releases that Brendon has been accepted by inconvertible evidence, by the DA, to be in fact, the killer of your daughter. All of this must have been a terrible blow to you folks. You have my deepest condolences. Are there any questions you have for me? About my rates, my background, or any point of law?" Leland had previously explained his rates over the telephone.

"Mr. Costello, only, what you think it's all about. Do you think the police may arrest Myrna or myself? We are satisfied to put ourselves in your hand, if you are willing to help us."

"No problem on that account. I will take your case. But please call me Lee. No need for formalities. Do you mind if I call you Ed?"

"That sounds fine Lee."

"Now to answer your question. The circumstances you have mentioned are very thin for a probable cause warrant. The way the law works is, that the police, when investigating a crime, and stumbles upon a suspect, they must obtain a warrant for his or her arrest. They must have credible probable cause evidence, to obtain the warrant, which must be signed by a judge. They can only arrest a suspect without a warrant, when the suspect is apprehended in the act of the crime. They may detain a person of interest under certain circumstances, and apply for the warrant secondarily. This would be particular, with

(112)

the fear of flight from the person suspected, or some ongoing danger to the public, or to the suspect, him or herself. So, to answer your question, I do not believe they have enough to hold you as yet. They need something more tangible. Be sure to contact me first, if you find your revolver. I would want to be there when it is tested for ballistics. You need to consider the custody of the gun. You need to be sure that it has not fallen into the hands of anybody else. You need not tell me, if you are guilty or not of the crime. That would only be necessary, should you want to make a confession. You are free to confide in me, any part you may have played in the crime. Under law, I cannot divulge to the authorities or any other person that information. That is attorney-client privilege. It does constrain me to abide by certain ethics as we progress, should it come to that."

Edward looked over to Myrna, then turned back to Lee, and told him, they had said, all they know about the whole affair.

"That's fine. Now it is just a waiting game, to see if they will be wanting to bring you in for those interviews. Should that occur, I will accompany you and guide you through the entirety of the deposition."

Ed and Myrna felt relieved. They accepted, that they were in good hands. Lee had given them the moral support they needed. He seemed to have a certain positive attitude, that made them feel secure. The nightmare took a short reprieve.

The following day, Thursday, a break in the Brendon case came bursting into the police station. An elderly man came in to speak with the detectives working on the Brendon murder case. His name was Joe Flynn. He was a retiree and lived two blocks down from Karen Morgan's house on 24th Ave. He was working in his front yard, trimming the bushes when he stumbled across a .38 caliber pistol. He had heard about the killing up the street. He thought the gun might be important. As it turned out, it certainly was.

Joe Flynn was ushered back to Brad and Matt's office. Both detectives were at their side by side desks. "This gentleman has something, you might want to see." The clerk left the man to meet with the officers.

Brad; "What do you have there?" The man was holding a shoebox. But the content was not shoes. It was the pistol he had discovered in his hedge. "I found this gun in my bushes in the front yard of my house. I was trimming this morning and it was wedged right in there. I live on Bristol Ave about two blocks from Karen Morgan. I thought this might be connected to that shooting a few weeks ago."

Brad and Matt became very interested in their morning caller. Brad asked to see the gun. The shoe box was handed to him. Matt became busy taking notes. He jotted down the man's name and address. Brad opened the box and was exposed to a shiny Smith and Wesson .38 special caliber revolver. It was an 'L' model with a four-inch barrel. A model that came out in the early 1980s. "You say this was lodged in your shrubs?"

"Yes, it was. I was clipping and there it was. I was dumbfounded. Then, I got to thinking of that young man being shot up the street. I figured the gun might be involved."

"That's certainly a possibility. I want to thank you for turning it in. We will run tests on it to determine whether or not it was the weapon in the homicide. If it proves to be such, we will need to keep it for evidence. If not, an advertisement will be run for lost and found. If no-one claims it in ninety days you can file a claim for it."

"No thanks. I have no need for a gun. Too many out there as is."

After completing the interview with Joe, and having his fingerprints taken, so as to eliminate any prints of his, that showed up, when the gun was later dusted for prints, Brad and Matt rushed to the gun lab, where the gun could be fired into a tank of water. The retrieved bullets then would be checked for the barrel-markings, to be matched with the bullets taken from Wade's body. Brad had Sergeant Debra Langley run a data check on the serial numbers of the weapon. Oregon does not have a registration requirement of firearms. However, points of sale could lead to the original, and possibly subsequent purchasers of the gun. Gun stores in particular, made records of all handgun sales. A background search was required before delivery, on any hand gun sold, only at gun-show type of sale venues. Gun dealers were bound to open inspection by the authorities. They were required to keep records of all sales and report to the state. Oregon is considered one of the more lenient states when it comes to ownership and sales.

Two results were ascertained by the double checking of the gun. First, there was a positive matchup of the ammo fired from the newly discovered pistol, and the three bullets taken from Wade's corpse. Secondly, the gun was traced to the original buyer from a gun store in Eugene. The buyer was recorded as Benjamin Smiley. The purchase was made in 1982.

"Well matt, we are off to the races now. We might be getting close to solving this case."

(115)

"I agree. We have the weapon for sure. Now to track the owner or owners as the case may be."

"We have the address for Smiley. He lives in the south hills in Springfield. Up on Bendix Drive. That would be one of those high scale homes overlooking Mt. Pisgah."

Brad and Matt made the drive to Smiley's home on Bendix Drive, Thursday afternoon. Brad was right. It was a very high scale house. Most likely in the million-dollar range. It looked big enough for three families. The view from the westside veranda was breathtaking. A wonderful view of the very popular Mt. Pisgah. The mountain is small for a mountain, but large for a hill. It is very popular with outdoor enthusiasts. A very popular hiking site. And the veranda is where the two detectives ended up with their host.

"So, gentlemen, what do you think of the view?"

"Spectacular", replied Matt.

"That's what sold me on the place, twenty years ago. It's a bit bigger than we need, Linda and I. We have two boys, but they have been on their own, for longer than I care to remember. Of course, they do come for visits with their little ones in tow. Officers, what brings you to my home? I am sure it has to do with more than the grand view."

Brad; "Mr. Smiley, we are here to check on a gun you purchased many years ago. It's a Smith and Wesson .38 special. Do you still own the gun?"

"That's a long story. But in brief the answer is no. You see, I bought that pistol as a gift for a friend of mine at the time. I haven't seen it since."

"Can you tell us, who you gave it to?"

"Of course. I used to manage Hyde/Perkins Heavy Equipment in Glenwood. The company is still there in business. Much to my surprise. Back in the day, I thought I was totally indispensable to the existence of the company. However, after I retired from managing the company, it went right along without me. Of course, I am happy to see they are still prospering. But it does put me in my place. You know, the old saying, no one is indispensable. Now, about the gun. As I said, I bought it for a friend. Eddy Struthers came into the shop one day, about five years after I had become manager. He was looking for a sales job. He was a very impressive young man. I think, I took a liking to him right off. He was full of energy and high spirits. Well, I hired him right there on the spot. I put him into training with one of our sales reps. It turned out to be a good call. Within a month, he was hell on wheels. Within a couple of months, he was our top salesman. He and I gradually became good buddies. We hit the town together, did some fishing together, bowling, you name it. We were good friends. I introduced him to firearms. We would go to the pistol range and work the targets. About two months of target practice and he outscored me. So, as reward, I gave him the gun, I had lent him for shooting at the range. It was a .38 special Smith and Wesson. That would have been over twenty years ago. We stayed close friends even after he married Myrna. Then along came Alexis, poor soul. We were still close buddies, even though we cut back on our drinking around town. Then a couple years later the damnable thing happened. Myrna came down with cancer of the uterus. It was stage one and she had the operation to remove a small tumor. The doctors said at the time that the prognosis was excellent. She had to do some radiation treatment, but in the end, she was deemed cured. That was certainly a relief, but there is more to it. Eddy was so shaken up, he took to praying every day and night. He became convinced, that the prayers were heard, and God had intervened in saving his precious wife. He was never quite the same after that. He took up the religion. That was fine and dandy. Putting himself in good with the Lord. But it began to put a strain on our relationship. I am not an atheist. But on the other hand, I am not a holy roller. Church became his sole interest. It was hard to be around him. It wasn't so much as preaching to everybody, but it always came around to Jesus, and how much he cares for everyone. It gets to be pretty much. As I said, it put a strain on our buddying together. A year or two later the old magic was gone completely. I still respected him, and it didn't interfere with his production on the job up until his retirement. We stayed friends, but just not like before. That's probably a bit more than you wanted to hear, but I felt you should know the whole story. As far as I know, he may still have the pistol. Of course, he may have sold it or given it away."

Brad pulled a photo and showed it to Benjamin. "Is this the gun you gave him?"

"Yes. It looks like it. Of course, I can't say without a doubt, that is it. I suppose the gun was used in a shooting. Maybe even murder?"

"Mr. Smiley, I thank you for your time and help. I would ask that you keep this meeting on the quite for a while. We are in the middle of an investigation, of Wade Brendon's homicide, and some information, is best held close to the breast. This particular gun may or may not be involved. We won't know until we further investigate."

As soon as the detectives left his house, Ben made a quick telephone call to his friend. "Hello Eddy. How is everything?"

"Ben, is that you? I'm surprised to hear from you.

(118)

It's been ages. I want to thank you for the nice card you sent for Alexis. I know you would have been at the services had you been in the country at the time."

"Yes. You can be sure of that. I regret that we were away at the time. Linda and I had just flown out Friday, the day before her death. We had a three-week vacation in China and other Asian countries. I didn't find out until we returned home. It was quite a buzz. I was terribly shocked. I'm calling you in reference to a visit, I just had from Eugene Police detectives. They have found a pistol that resembles the one I gave you many years ago. It was on the records, as being the one I bought. They wanted to know if I still owned it. I didn't mean to throw you under the bus, but I couldn't do other, than to tell them, I had given it to you back in the 80s. I suspect you have either sold it or given it away."

"Ben, I appreciate you calling me about it."

"Listen Ed, don't say another word about it. Don't tell me anything. If this is something, that ends up in a trial or some such, it's better for you and me, if I don't know anything. I just wanted to alert you about the police call on me. I'm sure, no matter what it's all about, that your hands are clean."

"How is everything at home? How is Linda and all those grandkids?

"Couldn't be any better. Everyone is fine and healthy. Let me know, if there is anything I can do to help. I think it is prudent, that you hire an attorney."

"I'm happy to hear everything is good at home. About the attorney, we have already got one on board. We have been interviewed by the police. Everything will work out fine. Please don't trouble yourself over any of this."

(119)

"I just wanted you to know, I still think of you as a friend."

"Same here, Ben. You take care."

Brad and Matt drove back to headquarters. In their office, they began to mull over the new evidence with the Chief. "Brad, this is beginning to add up to trouble for Edward Struthers. And possibly his wife," Matt exclaimed.

"I agree wholeheartedly. It looks like we have substantial probable cause to go for a warrant. I don't like it, but as you say it all begins to add up. We have the weapon, we have motive, and the right colored car at the scene. It's enough to make the case look solid against the Struthers. Or at least one of them.

Chief Burrows; "There is no doubt that we have the goods. At least for the arrest. If the folks are innocent, let's hope they can come up with plausible counter explanations. Particularly about the gun. Brad, take it to the DA and let them make the call on the warrant. By the way, did we get any prints off the pistol?"

"Yes and no Chief. We weren't able to get any prints other than those of the man, that found it in his yard. All other prints were too smudged and covered by Flynn's prints. He didn't use careful protocol in handling the gun. The gun was discarded quickly after the shooting, there would not have been time to wipe it clean. Too bad about Flynn's handling of it. I think it was thrown in some sort of panic right after the shooting."

"That seems to make sense. Once you get your warrant, it's time we bring them in and began the process."

Brad and Matt made the short trip to the DA's office. Once in the room with the Deputy District Attorney, Brad laid out the evidence file, showing Edward and Myrna

Struthers, as suspects in the slaying of Wade Brendon.

"Gentlemen, this is enough goods to make a warrant for suspicion of felony homicide. Whether its Murder 1 or lessor, to be determined later. We should be able to have the warrant in hand in a few shakes. You'll have it on your data base within the hour. Bring them in."

Brad and Matt stopped at Shari's for a quick bite It was shortly after one PM. They had their sandwich and cup of pea soup. Pie was an option. Shari's is well renowned for their pies. Apparently, their startup was as a pie shop. Hard to resist. However today the detectives waived off the dessert portion of lunch.

After lunch, and in Brad's unmarked police car, Brad engaged the dashboard computer and dialed up the database, for his expected warrant. It was there all signed and official. He aimed his vehicle in the direction of the Strother's residence.

"Matt, this one of the most difficult arrests, I have ever made. I don't relish it one bit. Down deep, I hope we are wrong. I mean, I hope there is a flaw in the evidence."

"Yeah. I know what you mean. Such seemingly nice folks. It's hard to think of somebody with their religious beliefs, could do anything as terrible as this."

"It's more complicated than that for me. It is a known fact that Wade killed their only child. It's hard not to think, that if one of them, or both, pulled the trigger on Wade, how do you judge such an action. I know revenge is not a legal excuse for murder. I wish it had been in self-defense. For that they could have gotten a medal. I know, I'm overthinking the whole thing. But it all smells to high heaven."

Two O'clock PM, Brad and Matt arrived at the Struthers' residence. Both Edward and Myrna were home.

It was a short visit. Brad advised Edward that he was under arrest for the murder of Wade Brendon. Myrna was arrested for complicity. He advised them to save any comments until their attorney was present. Restraints would not be utilized. They were politely led to the police car and settled in the back seat. "I am very sorry this has to be done, but there is just too much evidence, uncovered in our investigation, that gives us cause to believe you had a hand in Wade's death."

Edward; "We understand officer. You are only doing your duty. It will all be sorted out."

Brad was taken aback by the man's stoic response. It brought to mind his first encounter with Edward. The day the old man reacted cool and calm when told about his daughter's death. Then boom. He fell to the floor unexpectedly and was out like a light. His reaction just now, seems very aloof and almost unconcerned. A small misunderstanding, that would be straightened out in short time. It was somewhat surreal.

The couple were booked at county jail. They were given their Miranda rights and allowed to call their attorney.

(122)

Chapter 20   Getting Ready for Trial

Leland Costello got the call from his clients, booked in county jail. It was midafternoon. He got himself together and drove over to 5th street and entered the detention center. He was allowed to meet with the Struthers together, in an interview room. He had been given a copy of the arrest warrant. A DA information filing was not yet available.

"It doesn't look good Ed. They have the murder weapon used against Wade. They have tracked it to you. Please explain everything to me. I need to know the whole story. Did you have possession of the gun in question? Did you do the shooting? Remember what I told you about attorney/client privilege."

"The gun was given to me by an old friend many years ago. We used to do firing practice at the Baron indoor gun range. He was my boss at Hyde/Perkins Equipment. He taught me how to shoot. One day I outscored him, and he rewarded me with the pistol. As I say, we were very good friends back then."

"Did you sell or loose the gun later on?"

"No. I kept it all these years. Didn't do any more shooting. Just keep it in a cabinet."

"So, how do you, account for it being used in the Brendon homicide?"

"That, I cannot say. It's a total mystery to me. I haven't seen the gun for some time."

"There will be a hearing tomorrow. It is called the first appearance. You will be given the opportunity to make a plea. I'm assuming you wish to plead not guilty. Should you do so, then there is a thirty-day call period. That gives us time to do our own investigation and to make filings.

(123)

It also gives the DA an opportunity to take evidence to a grand jury. You are being held on a filing by the District Attorney. This is tantamount to an accusation. The judge will weigh the evidence provided in the information filing, and determine whether or not there is sufficiency for the prosecution to prevail in trial. That would mean, you would be confined until trial. It is very difficult to get bail on a murder rap. Myrna is charged with complicity. That's going to be a harder case for the prosecution. They have no witness to back that claim. I do not expect them to press that very far. I believe they will cut her free, and go after the murder rap. I'm afraid, all of this is going to take some time. These affairs play out over months, Sometimes years. I'm also afraid that there will be great costs to you. Murder trials can be very expensive. There is so much ground work, and research that must be done. For instance, I will need to learn what happened to the gun you once owned. It will be utmost important, that we can trace the weapon to the shooter. Or at least, find proof that the gun was no longer in your possession."

"So, we go before the judge tomorrow? We will both definitely plead innocent of the charges."

"Fair enough. I will meet you in the morning at the courthouse. We will be allowed to confer before the proceedings begin. I will be by your side, when the charges are read. The entire proceedings will be short. The charges will be read and you will be asked to make your plea. It's the first step in a long ordeal. I will do all in my power to obtain security release for you Ed. But don't rely on it much. As I have stated, it is rare to be bailed on a murder rap. Myrna, I will have you back home before you know it."

Friday went as expected. Leland represented the Struthers at their first arraignment. The proceedings were based on an information filing by the District Attorney. The defendants were asked separately how they plead. Each plead not guilty. Leland moved that the charges against Myrna be dropped as the information provided by the DA, showed no probable cause, as there were no witnesses to her involvement with any crime. The DA answered, that circumstances were strongly pointing to her involvement. Since that involvement could not be specifically defined, the judge ruled, that she was to be set free. He stated that the prosecution could re-charge, if they were able to obtain an indictment from a grand jury. Myrna was released. Edward would be incarcerated until further court proceedings. This meant that he would be behind bars until a grand jury handed down an indictment. The judge ruled that there was sufficient evidence provided in the information filing, that would most likely lead to a favorable prosecution of the charges. In Oregon, a trial must be preceded by a grand jury indictment. The information filing is merely a primer, setting things in motion. After indictment, the initial arraignment would be repeated.

Wednesday of the following week, the indictment for Edward Struthers charged with felony homicide, was handed down by the grand jury. This is known, as a true bill in legal terms. It simply means that the jurors found, that there was sufficient evidence to send the matter to trial for prosecution.

The prosecution did not open a grand jury, in the matter of complicity by Myrna Struthers. That would be delayed until further investigation demanded it.

Leland made a couple more visits to county detention

(125)

to visit with his client. He had not formulated his defense strategy as yet. Edward remained unbendable in his assertion, that he knew nothing about the murder. He could not account for his gun being used in the murder. Leland also talked with Myrna at her home. There seemed to be a problem with her recollections of Saturday morning of Brendon's killing. She told Leland, that Ed had acted strange that morning. He had been gone for almost an hour that morning. When he came back into the house with the morning paper, she had asked where he had been. He replied, "been? I haven't been anywhere. I just went out to pick up the paper."

"I thought it was awfully peculiar. But he didn't bat an eye. He said, I must be imagining things. He sat down and read the paper. I thought, he was probably right. It was just my imagination."

Leland was beginning to see that there was something screwy about this case. Somebody was lying. Perhaps they were both lying. Perhaps one or both were nuts. That thought lit an idea in his head. There just might be something, to the notion that Edward was off his rocker. He had even spooked his wife that morning. Leland began to think of his next move. He would need to bring in a specialist to examine his client.

"Was there any other incident that made you wonder about your husband?"

"Only, that when the officers first came to the house, He fainted right away and fell to the floor."

Friday, the day after visiting Myrna, Leland made contact with a local Doctor of Psychiatry. Her name was Lenora Freeman. She was nationally recognized in her treatment of Dissociative Identity Disorder (DID). He was able to encourage her to see his client at county.

(126)

She would make the first call that afternoon.

Leland met Dr. Freeman in the lobby of Lane County Detention Center. He spent ten minutes with her, going over his client's dilemma. They entered the interview room, where Edward had been brought into beforehand. Leland introduced the doctor to Edward. It had crossed Lenora's mind that her most important case of DID was also named Eddy.

"Hello Edward. My name is Lenora. May I call you Ed?"

"Certainly. I take pride in not hogging the alphabet for my moniker." He smiled broadly and sincerely.

"Leland has told me about your problems. I am so sorry about you losing your daughter. I know that is a terrible loss."

"Yes. It is. It's a test of our faith. All things are known to God. His reasoning is not to be questioned. That is the hardest part of our test. Terrible pain is hard to reckon with."

"How do you feel about that? Do you feel, you are meeting the challenge of that test?"

"If you mean, do I still put my faith in the Lord, the answer is yes."

Lenora met with Edward for an hour. Her probing was noninvasive. More like two friends chatting with each other. She wanted to lay the foundation of trust and bonding. She would meet with him over the next two weeks, half a dozen times. After the third session, she was able to utilize hypnotherapy. After three sessions of hypnotherapy, she was able to make a report on her conclusions. They were troubling.

Leland met with her in her office on Broadway, downtown Eugene.

(127)

"Well Doctor. Do we have a sick man on our hands?"

"If by sick, you mean mentally disturbed, I am afraid we do."

"Does that mean, you find him to be legally mentally defective?"

"You must keep in mind I am a psychiatrist not a lawyer. I do not deal in legal terms. If the legal question is, did he do a criminal act, such as homicide, and know right from wrong, the answer is going to be very complicated. In his normal state of mind, he has high religious values, and certainly knows right from wrong. However, I believe if he committed the homicide, he is charged with, he would have been under the stress of irresistible urge."

"Does that mean, he did the shooting, knowing it was wrong, but was so compelled that he could not avoid the act?"

"I'm afraid it is more complicated than that. I have worked with the patient, using hypnotherapy, during three one-hour sessions. I have coaxed him back to that fateful Saturday morning. At that point; I was up against a mental block-out. His mind has completely blocked out his activities that morning. He recalls going out of the house only to fetch the morning newspaper. He cannot account nor remember his actions for the period of time he left the house. In his mind, he simply stepped outside to pick up the paper. He was not being deceitful, when he told his wife that he had not been anywhere away from the house. The symptoms suggest PTSD. This would easily be attributed to the traumatic loss of his daughter. He is a religious man, and spent much time in solemn prayer. His praying was in fact, a search for peace and understanding.

(128)

Much like self-medicating. My probing, indicates to me, that there grew a tremendous conflict. His religious beliefs, and relying on the tenets of the Christian bible, came into conflict with his hatred for the killer of Alexis. It was so great that he demanded of himself, retribution by his own hands. The end result manifested such confusion in his mind, that he fell into a catatonic state. That would be similar to sleep walking. His brain set itself on auto-pilot. He would have been focusing on one thing only. The eradication of the killer of his daughter. You might think of it as a robotic setting, with one purpose programmed in. He would have completed the job with or without witnesses. So, as you can see, in this scenario, at the time of the shooting, there was no cognizance process, of whether the act was right or wrong. Merely a job that had to be performed. Once the shooting was finished, he simply would have driven away. This would explain why he threw the gun away in such close proximity to the crime. It would be the same as throwing away a piece of litter, no longer of any use. Once back in his own driveway, and approaching the house, he most likely began to come out of his sleepwalking, found the paper on the lawn and picked it up. His brain, now off of auto-pilot, could in no way account for the lost time."

"Wow. That is some psychological maze running. How determined, are you that this is the true gist of it? Can you be one hundred percent sure of your findings?"

"If you mean, could the patient be play-acting? That is beyond any reasonable doubt, not the case. It would take a tremendously devious and trained mind, to outwit hypnotherapy. I stand by my diagnosis. Whether or not, he shot Mr. Brendon is still up for grabs."

(129)

Leland met with the Deputy District Attorney, Oliver Stoltz. Oliver was the highest-ranking Deputy in the DA's office. He would often be the prosecutor for high profile cases. He had been assigned the Strother's murder case.

Leland had in his files, the written summary of Dr. Freeman's study of the indicted, Edward Struthers.

"I thought you should see this Oliver. I will be moving for an acquittal on the homicide indictment, due to mental defect. Dr. Freeman's examination, and hypnotherapy sessions with the defendant, clearly illustrate his incapacity. This does not imply that he was the shooter."

"I see. Give me a few minutes to run through your report. Would you like some coffee while you wait?"

"No. I'm good. Take your time. I think you will find it interesting reading."

Five minutes went by as Oliver read the Doctor's file. He let the paper down on his desk and looked across at Leland. "It's a very interesting scenario. But I don't see how it is possible to determine from her sessions with the defendant, that she could be so sure of her diagnosis. I take it, there has been no other treatment by the good doctor of the suspect. I cannot imagine, a person leaving his home with a loaded gun, getting into an automobile, driving across town, pulling up to the curb, rolling down the car window, and calmly firing three rounds into a man leaving his house for his car. Then driving back across town to his own home, after throwing the weapon into a hedge, Then, magically waking up, as he is going through the door. I don't think a jury will buy it either."

The two attorneys chatted more about the case and the mental defect or lack there-of, of Edward Struthers.

"It would seem a better outcome for your client, would be to consider pleading down to murder two.

You have the crime of passion defense to be considered. I don't see it going any lower than that. Twenty-five with possibility of parole, he could be out in twelve."

"Hell, Oliver. That, would be tantamount to life, considering his age. He would most likely die in prison."

"That's the breaks. You do the crime, you serve the time. Listen, don't think, I have no sympathy for the man. I can no way condone his actions. However, the murder of his daughter certainly screws things a bit. I really think you should consider plea bargaining. See what we can work out."

"No. That, I will not do to my client. We'll face the jury. Let them sort it out. However, you have my discovery, expect an argument on mental defect."

Chapter 21   Trial

Attorney Leland Costello had filed a brief with the court which was also directed to the DA's office. The brief called for a pre-trial hearing regarding the mental condition of his client. A hearing was granted the following week. The Deputy District Attorney was well prepared. Oliver Stoltz had wasted no time after the interview with Leland, in his office. He had arranged for a psychiatric review of the suspect. A three-hour session was held with the detainee, and a psychiatrist from State Mental Hospital. A copy of the report was sent to Leland as part of prosecution's discovery. In trial matters, all sides were made privy to the cards being held by one another. It's a different kind of poker game. A game that did not allow showboating or last-minute surprises.

The pretrial hearing was held. Arguments were made by the DA and defense. The written reports had been made available to the judge. In the end, the ruling was that not enough evidence was substantiated to support the legal terms of mental defect. The issue could be settled by the jury.

A jury panel of seven women and five men were selected. Alternates were also selected in the event any juror should need to be dismissed. Leland was satisfied, with the selection. A heavy sided woman to man ratio, would tend to show more compassion. Trial was set to commence on September 18, 2017. The state would be first at bat. Opening arguments by the prosecution was short. The facts derived from the Eugene Police Department were displayed to the jury. The charges had been refined to murder two. Prosecution knew there would be too much consideration, for the emotions of a man revenging the death of his daughter. If convicted, Edward faced a possibility of twenty -five years in prison. Most definitely a life sentence.

Leland had decided to push hard for an acquittal based on mental defect. He made this abundantly clear in his opening rebuttal statements to the jury. There would be no defense based on, who in fact shot Wade Brendon. That was a matter for the state, to prove beyond a shadow of doubt .Leland had considered justifiable homicide as the primary defense. Eugene/Springfield had seen two such cases in the last twenty years. In one incident, a father walked into a McDonalds Restaurant with a gun in hand. He walked up behind a man and shot him at close range. The victim was dead on the spot. The shooting was predicated on the fact, that the victim had threatened his daughter with deadly harm. It was some sort of fracas over a bad drug deal. The case never went to a grand jury. The DA dismissed any charges against the father as justifiable homicide. In a second case, a man burglarized another man's car on West 11th Street. The car owner caught him in the act. The robber ran from the scene. The car owner, who happened to be a black belt Karate expert, chased the man for two blocks and opened fire with a hand gun. The fleeing criminal was shot in the back and died on the street. The DA also ruled justifiable homicide. It would seem, that the Struthers case could have been taken in the same light. However, times change, and with different values of the changing times, it was not to be. Edward was charged and indicted by a grand jury, for murder two.

In his opening arguments, Leland stressed that this was not a simple case of murder. In this case, the defendant was clouded in a stigmatized state of shock. He would offer testimony, that would clearly show that his

(133)

client was suffering from mental disorders, at the time of the shooting, conditions so severe, that Edwards Struthers was totally mentally incapacitated. He had no cognizant control over his actions.

With the jury in place and opening arguments completed, the state began its prosecution. The first witness was Detective Brad Ferguson. After being sworn in and giving his name, address, and occupation, the questioning began.

Stoltz; "Detective Ferguson, were you involved in the investigation of the Wade Brendon homicide?"

"Yes. I am the lead detective on the case."

"Detective, did you make the arrest of the defendant?"

"Yes. I made the arrest based on a warrant for suspicion of homicide. My partner, Matt Wagner was with me at the time."

"Was the defendant showing any signs of distress or agitation at time of arrest?"

"No. He was very calm and co-operative. "

"Did you have any encounter with the defendant before the arrest?"

"Yes. On three occasions. The first time was the morning his daughter was murdered. I went to his home to inform him in person, of the tragedy. Matt was with me on that occasion. The second encounter was at Wade Brendon's funeral. I did a third interview with him at his home."

"Did you observe any unusual behavior on those three occasions?"

"On the first meeting, after I relayed the sad news of his daughter's death, that very morning, he was extremely calm at first, but within a few seconds, he fainted dead

(134)

out. He came to a couple of minutes later. Matt and I, had lifted him onto the sofa. The next two times, there was nothing remarkable in his behavior."

"Now, let us refer to the arrest warrant. What evidence had you uncovered, to substantiate getting the warrant signed by a judge?"

"There were three items which we submitted. One; was the matching color of the defendant's car, to one reported by a witness, as being driven from the scene of the shooting. Two; there was sufficient evidence of the defendant's hatred for the victim. Three; and most compelling of all, was the tracing of defendant's handgun to proximity of the killing."

Stoltz; "Your honor, I would like to refer to prosecution's evidence marked item A-1, the handgun submitted as the weapon used in the shooting of Wade Brendon." Oliver picked up the gun and handed it to Brad on the witness stand. "Is this the very weapon you retrieved from the vicinity of the crime scene?"

"It is. However, if I may elaborate, the pistol was discovered in a front yard hedge by the landowner. It was discovered two weeks after the shooting, by Joe Flynn, the landowner, while he was trimming his hedge. He immediately turned it in to my office."

"Two questions. First; how were you able to determine ownership of the gun? And two; how can you be sure, that the gun was the same gun used in the killing?"

"We were able to track the gun to the original purchaser. This is a man living in Springfield, a Mr. Benjamin Smiley. This was easy to do. All firearms have serial numbers. In this state, all purchases are recorded and filed with the state. Everything is in a data base.

We made a match of the serial number with the sale made to Mr. Smiley. As far as identifying the gun, as the murder weapon; again, it is very simple and scientific. All firearms are manufactured in such a way, that the barrel interiors are grooved win a spiraling, minutely notched interior. This causes the ammo to spiral as it travels through the barrel. The result gives greater accuracy to the projectile as it leaves the barrel. All firearms have individual identifiable grooving patterns. Bullets that have been fired, can be compared one to another, by markings on the spent shell. They carry the signature of the very gun that fired them. To ascertain if two separate bullets were fired from the same gun, it is a matter of comparing the groove markings. This process is done under microscope. We matched bullets taken from the body of the victim, to bullets fired into a water tank in our lab, from the gun in question. There was a positive match. It was the same gun as used in the killing."

"You have taken photos at the scene of the shooting? Are these three photographs, taken by your team at the time of your original investigation of the scene? Your honor, I refer to exhibit A-2, A3, and A4." Stoltz showed the photographs to Brad. He also displayed them to the jury.

Brad; "Yes. These are our photos taken in the beginning of our investigation at the crime scene."

"Was there a determination made, as to the distance from the shooter to the victim?"

"Yes. It was determined that the shooter was approximately sixty feet away from the victim."

"Was there a finding of pattern to the entry wounds on the victim?"

"Yes. The bullets were spaced in an arching line, no more than four inches apart. One was dead center to the heart."

"Would you consider this the work of a marksman?"

"I would say so. At least, someone who was very proficient with handguns."

"No more questions."

Judge; "Defense do you wish to cross examine the witness?"

"Yes, your honor." As Leland approached the center of the room facing Brad. He stood by the edge of the table assigned to his team. "Officer Ferguson, you have concluded, that the defendant was the only person, that could have used the gun that Saturday morning? Are there any loopholes in that line of thinking? Is it possible the gun might have been somehow misplaced and ended up, in who knows who's hands? Did you obtain any fingerprints from the gun?"

Brad; "I do not make conclusions. I leave that up to the court and the jury. I simply gather evidence and submit it to the system. We do not have fingerprint evidence. The only clear prints are those of Mr. Flynn."

"Then, what you are testifying to, is simply, the last known ownership of the weapon. Is that true?"

"I am testifying to my investigation, and the evidence I gathered. We are sure, that Mr. Struthers was the last known owner of the weapon."

"You have testified, that Mr. Struthers showed certain strains when you advised him of his daughter's death. Did you take the impression, that there was something troublesome about his demeanor?"

Stoltz; "Objection your honor. Officer Ferguson is not

(137)

trained to parse people's mental state. Prosecution will bring forth a qualified doctor of psychiatry, to cover the issue of state of mind."

Leland; "Your honor, asking about a person's demeanor does not require any more training, than I am sure, this officer deals with on a daily basis. The prosecution has already opened the door to this line of questioning"

"Objection over ruled. You may answer the question. Keep your testimony in layman's terms. Do not try to analyze."

"The man was shaken as I have testified. At first, he was very calm. It was about two minutes later when he collapsed to the floor. The fainting seemed natural enough. I suppose, the time elapse was a new experience for me. It wasn't only the time delay; it had to do with his extreme calmness in his first acceptance of the fact of his daughter's death. There were no immediate signs of disturbance. He was very calm and serene at first. Then like a flash, he fell fainted to the floor. When he revived two minutes later, there was that same composure as if nothing had happened. When I asked, if there was anything I could do, he answered that his preacher would come and help him and his wife."

"To this date, are there any other persons of interest in this case? Anybody else that you may be tracking?"

"As far as the department is concerned, this case is closed pending the outcome of this trial."

"In other words, if Mr. Struthers is found guilty, the case is closed?"

"That would put an end to the file, yes."

Leland finished his questioning of Brad. The next witness for the prosecution was Doctor Michael Shelby of

(138)

the state hospital.

As a matter of Voir Dire, Stoltz established the Doctors expertise; "Doctor Shelby, please give the court your name, address. and a brief resume."

The doctor gave his full name, address, and his background of twenty-four years of practice, eight of which, were as resident at the state mental hospital in Salem.

"So, Doctor, it is fair to say, that you are well qualified in the field of psychoanalyses?"

"I am familiar with symptoms of mental illness or defects. I have treated a wide range of disorders, in my lifetime of service."

"Doctor, have you had an opportunity to examine the defendant, Edward Struthers?"

"Yes. I was requested by the court to examine the man."

"And you have filed a report of your findings?"

"Yes. I filed a full report of my examination."

"Your honor, I submit as evidence, the ten-page report marked as Exhibit B-2, which has been given in deposition with defendant's council in attendance."

Stoltz to the witness; "In your report as submitted, you claim to have not uncovered any abnormal or deviant mental defect?"

"That is a true brief summary. However, there is noted, that Mr. Struthers has exhibited a high level of stress. I attribute that to two things primarily. First; would be the grief over the loss of his daughter. Secondly; the weight of his current dilemma. These are each, cursors that can cause turmoil to a person's state of mind."

"This court will be highly concerned with his state of mind. Would you conclude, that the defendant ever acted,

(139)

or carried out any action, without full cognizance of those actions? If he did an evil act, would he have known right from wrong?"

"Mr. Struthers is a very moral man of high ethics. This is due primarily to his religious faith. His Christian values are very demanding of him, to do what is right. Not only right by law, but to his higher calling."

"So, what you are saying is, he would definitely know right from wrong?"

"Most definitely."

"Please, if you would, explain the meaning of irresistible impulse."

"Irresistible impulse is a common symptom. It occurs in a high number of individuals. The first time a young man or woman kisses for the first time, may be the results of a strong irresistible urge or impulse. It is not a mental defect of any kind. The only time it is dangerous, is when you might be standing on a precipice and have a compulsion to jump off the edge. This is also fairly common. Thankfully, the urge is not strong enough to overcome fear and reason. In medical terms, irresistible urge is only problematic when coupled with some extreme paranoia. If a person happened to be undergoing a psychotic disorder, such as paranoia or schizophrenia; there could be dire consequence. In such cases, intervention would be necessary."

"Did you find any symptoms of either, of the mentioned disorders in the defendant?"

"No. In fact, much the opposite. He shows signs of peace and serenity in his demeanor, which I find extraordinary, given the stress I have noted."

"Thank you Doctor for your help"

(140)

Leland stood and addressed the Doctor. "Doctor Shelby, how much time in total, did you spend with the defendant?"

"That would be an aggregate of three hours."

"Were the sessions held in clinic or at detention?"

"The three sessions were each held at county detention center."

"Did you perform hypnotherapy during any of these sessions?"

"No, I did not. I employed standard methodology. The most common methods of evaluation."

"Would you give any credence, to an examination done by a nationally known Doctor of Psychiatry, if it was performed, using hypnotherapy?"

Stoltz; "Your honor, I object. The question is without foundation and goes beyond cross examination. If defense has such an examination, let him produce it in defense's case. The question as framed, is purely speculative with too many unknown variables."

"Objection sustained. Councilor, you will have opportunity to present your case, and any examinations that are applicable. You will then have the opportunity to recross the witness."

Leland; "Thank you Doctor. That will be all for now."

"Prosecution calls Mr. Benjamin Smiley."

Mr. Smiley setting in the courtroom, arose and approached the witness stand.

"Mr. Smiley, please state your name and address."

Smiley gave his full name and address.

"Mr. Smiley, are you acquainted with the defendant?"

"Yes. For more than thirty years."

"Please explain the nature of your relationship."

(141)

"We worked together at Hyde/Perkins Heavy Equipment. I was the manager, and he was one of our sales reps. I'm the one that hired him."

"Did you have a friendly relationship with him?"

"Yes, I did. For over thirty years. We used to hang together quite a bit. We had mutual activities that we shared."

"I notice you used the word 'had'. Has your relationship changed over the years?"

"Well, we both got married. That cut back on our carousing together. We kept up our bowling, fishing, target shooting, and hiking. Like I said, we had mutual interests on how to spend our off-time. Things did change after his wife came down with cancer. That's when he became a born-again Christian. He fell into a heavy believer. Our activities together fell off. We remained good friends until this day. We do not visit that much since retirement, but I still consider him a dear friend."

"Did you at one time, give to the defendant a Smith and Wesson .38 Special caliber hand gun?"

"Yes. Back in the eighties, we would target shoot over at Barons indoor shooting range. I let him use the .38. After a while he became pretty good. He beat my pants off one day. So, as a reward, I gave the gun to him."

"Can you identify the gun as the one entered into evidence?" As Stoltz handed the empty pistol to the witness.

"This is definitely the one."

"Can you be definitely sure? I mean there were thousands of this model manufactured."

"Yes, I am sure. You see, the manufacturers give each gun a serial number. That number was recorded with the state at time of purchase. The police have checked the

(142)

numbers and they match the one I bought."

"And was that the only Smith and Wesson .38 Special caliber gun you owned?"

"Yes, it was."

Stoltz; "Your honor, I call Joseph Flynn."

Joseph Flynn took the stand and was asked about finding the gun in his front yard hedge. He was also asked the proximity of his home to that of Karen Morgan up the street. He related how he found the gun upon trimming his hedge, and gave the distance from his house to Karen's. it was approximately two city blocks.

As with Smiley, there were no questions from defense.

The next witness was the County Medical Examiner. His testimony gave explicit details of the condition of the victim's body, when sent to the morgue. The ensuing autopsy revealed three bullet wounds. All three bullets were extracted from the body, and turned over to Eugene Police Department, as evidence in the homicide investigation. Death was caused instantaneously, by one bullet to the heart. Photographs were displayed as prosecution's exhibits C-I through four. Defense excused the witness without further query.

Stoltz; "Prosecution rests."

Judge; "Very well. It is eleven thirty. We shall adjourn until one PM. Councilor will you be ready to present defense by that time?"

"Yes, your honor. We are prepared and ready to call witnesses."

Leland had lunch with Dr. Lenora Freeman, his star witness. He realized that his only chance for acquittal would be, that of mental defect. "Well Doctor, you heard the testimony of states expert psychologist. Do you feel good about being able to counter his claims?"

"His report on Edward's condition is not necessarily misguided. I believe his findings were premature. I do not think, he spent enough time with the subject. He seemingly, approached the problem as an overseer, with the only object in mind, being to certify the mental condition of the subject. In my opinion, my study was more in depth. Especially with the hypnotherapy treatments. I approached the task as, the need to treat a patient. With this approach, my aim was to attempt to uncover any symptoms that might need attention."

"I believe you right down the line. We will lay out that thesis in my questioning. Be on your toes, when Stoltz takes his turn at you."

Chapter 22   Defense

One thirty, and the court room was packed. All the combatants were at their station. Only players not yet seated was the judge and the jury panel. This would be shortly rectified. The law clerk made his announcements as the judge entered from his chambers. All stood as the judge entered. They were quickly waved to be seated.

The judge started the proceeding by referring to two motions made by the defense. One; was pleading for the quashing of the evidence of the recovered gun. Leland had argued that it was prejudicial, and could not be conclusively shown that the defendant was the last in possession of the weapon.

The second motion, was to dismiss the charges based on insufficient factual evidence, and too much centered on circumstantial evidence. Both motions were denied.

The jury members, of twelve tried and true, were lead in after the judge made his response to the motions and were seated in the jury box.

Leland called his first witness. Mr. Avery Dirksen evangelist.

"Reverend Dirksen, you are an acquaintance of the defendant Mr. Struthers?"

"I have known Edward for about twenty years. He is a regular member of my congregation. He sits in services every Sunday for all that time, since I first ministered to him. He is a very devout believer. We prayed together, he, Myrna, and myself, the morning they lost their daughter."

"In all that time you have known Mr. Struthers, have you ever seen him display any hostility towards any other person?"

"No. Just the opposite. He has always shown human compassion towards his fellow man. Never even a word of anger or malice."

"Thank you, reverend. Thank you for coming."

Judge; "Prosecution?"

"Thank you, your honor. Reverend Dirksen, you are familiar with the Struthers' family as a whole, isn't that so?"

"Yes I am. They are all members of my flock. I have been to their home many times. I have dined with them. They are a part of my extended family."

"How would you characterize the relationship with Edward and his late daughter Alexis?"

"The Struthers are a close-knit family. They share their joy and their heartaches. As do I. Edward was extremely fond of his daughter. He was very proud of her. It was my pleasure to baptize her. I think that was the proudest day of his life."

"Would you say that he felt protective of her?

Leland; "I object to this line of questioning. It calls for a subjective opinion. Prosecution will have ample opportunity to explore any psychological reasoning, with my next witness, who is an expert in that field."

Judge; "You may want to rephrase your question, as to any physical manifestations, pertaining to what you are trying to reference."

"Did you ever see any act, that would emphasize his reaction to anyone, doing anything to harm his daughter?"

"Not that I can recall."

"No more questions."

Leland; "I call Doctor Lenora Freeman."

(146)

Lenora was sworn in land took her seat in the witness stand. She gave her name and address.

Leland questioned her regarding her resume as a certified psychiatrist. She gave her resume and her current practice history.

"Doctor, have you had an opportunity to examine the defendant?"

"The answer is yes, I have. That would be after his incarceration."

"Would you please explain the nature and results of your examination or examinations."

"I met with the patient for six one-hour sessions. After the initial three meetings, I applied psychotherapy. I find, that the patient is suffering from a variety of mental disfunctions. Primarily of which is PTSD. This is a fairly common disorder these days. It is especially found in military people, that have been exposed to extreme violence. Such as seeing others being mortally wounded. One case of seeing a friend killed, would be a strong factor. Seeing mass chaos of death and destruction amongst strangers would be another. In non-military situations, even civilians are vulnerable to the disorder, for instance, with the loss of a loved one. PTSD in and of itself can be treated with good prognosis. The problem with the defendant's case, comes from pressures from a couple of other disorders. These pressures arose out of identity complexities. The result was, that the defendant lost cognizance of his actions for a period of time. Time that he cannot relive or remember. I came to this conclusion, through the use of hypnotherapy. Under hypnosis, I was able to delve into his mind, right up to that period of time that the shooting of Mr. Brendon occurred. At that very point, there was a complete block out. He cannot account

(147)

for himself during a one-hour period that morning. Whatever he did that morning, was done in a somnambulistic state of mind."

"You are saying that he might have been sleepwalking?"

"That would be the shorthand version. It is a bit more complicated. It was more robotic. His actions would have been programmed into his mind. The various disorders made a perfect mental storm. His moral fiber being challenged by the trauma of loss. He is a praying man. Somehow his prayers did not satisfy the unrest turning in his mind. Action was called for. A call to action, he normally would not heed. This is when the identity disorder kicked in. His mind became subdued to the call, only after shutting down his mental awareness of reality. At this point, his mind would have been set on one action. He would be acting on irresistible impulse or urge.

"Doctor Freeman, how do you, account for the difference of the previous doctor's testimony?"

"I believe Doctor Shelby's approach to the situation differed from mine. Doctor Shelby met with the patient as a defendant on trial. His method of examining the man, was only to determine his faculty of mind. His sessions were half of the time, I spent with the patient. The important difference however was protocol. I approached the task, as I would in taking on a patient. My interest was to try to help the patient through any disorders, that I might uncover. I was aware, that it was my duty to report my findings."

"Is it then, in your findings, that Mr. Struthers is in dire need of mental health assistance?"

"I believe that Mr. Struthers needs a lengthy routine

(148)

of counseling. He does suffer mental disorders that could be cured with proper treatment."

"One last question Doctor. Again, if it should be proven without a doubt that Mr. Struthers did in fact shoot the victim, would he have been in a state of mind to differentiate right from wrong? Being under the stress of irresistible urge."

"Should the evidence be conclusive of he being the shooter, I maintain, that it would have occurred while Mr. Struthers' mind was operating on automatic mode. It would be left to his subconscious mind to determine right from wrong. At any rate, in this state of mind he would not be able to resist the preset objective. In the very least, his mind would have been very cloudy. It is very close in proximity to being self-hypnotized. The objective would be somewhat, like a post hypnotic suggestion."

"The witness is yours Mr. Stoltz."

"Good afternoon Doctor. I would like to start with your opinion, as opposed to the findings of Doctor Shelby. Do you find the doctor to be credible? Do you place a higher value on your credentials over his?"

"I have met the doctor in Salem. I am working for a client held in detention at the hospital. A very severe case. I have not worked in conjunction with Doctor Shelby. I am sure he is a very competent doctor. I do stand by my analysis. Possibly the time spent with patient has some bearing."

"You are being paid for your testimony by the defense?"

Leland; "Objection. I will withdraw my objection, if the prosecution will add 'as we have paid for our doctor's testimony'."

"I withdraw the question, your honor. Doctor please tell the court, whether a man, while under hypnosis, will act against his moral ethics?"

"Under normal conditions, no."

"Doesn't that imply, that the person would still know right behavior from wrong behavior?"

"Again, under normal conditions, yes. But please remember; here we are dealing with irresistible urge, and other mental disorders."

"Let's talk about the disorders. You seemed to have uncovered symptoms, that the state doctor did not. Is it true, that if a patient is examined by six different psychiatrists, that you might get six different diagnosis"?

"I believe that is something a humorist came up with. There are certainly different viewpoints, based on the background of each doctor involved. The differences in opinions are usually of a minor nature. Doctors of Psychiatry, usually are friendly to the notion of sharing viewpoints. That is working as a team in difficult situations. Psychiatry is a science. However not set in stone, as some other sciences. We are constantly discovering new disorders and methodology of treatment."

"So, what you are saying is, that it might have been better, had you and Doctor Shelby co-consulted with the defendant?"

"I think that is true. I am sure together, we could have compared notes, and come up with a consensus."

"You have testified, that you used hypnotherapy in your sessions with the defendant, is that true?"

"Yes. I used hypnosis in three one-hour sessions."

"You have just now testified, that your science is not set in stone. What about hypnotherapy? Is that set-in

(150)

stone? For instance, is it possible to be scammed by the patient?"

"It would take a very strong and devious mind, to be able to fool a doctor under those conditions. Being under, is almost impossible to fake to the trained physician."

"Is it also fair to say that many times, a doctor treating mental patients, may succumb to strong feelings of sympathy towards the patient, that may cloud their diagnosis. Especially, when that patient may be facing years of incarceration?"

Leland; "I strongly object to this question, and to the intended impugning of the witness. It's about the lowest, dirtiest trick, I have encountered in a court room with a trial of such consequence."

Judge; "I would not go so far as councilor. Of course, I have set through many more trials. I can certainly top the dirty trick portion of the objection. However, I do not see proper probative foundation for such a question. If prosecution intends to go in that direction, we may need to have a side bar.

"No, your honor. I am satisfied with the doctor's credentials. They speak for themselves. I will willfully withdraw the question. Doctor Freeman, I apologize for any hint that you are not one hundred percent ethical. Doctor, you have made your diagnosis presumably from one incident by the defendant. Is that sufficient to make the conclusions you have made?"

"There are other incidents, that I have reported in my statement to the court. Another example, could be taken from the testimony of Detective Ferguson. He has stated that the fainting spell, he encountered on reporting the murder of Mr. Struthers's daughter, was very unusual. That Mr. Struthers was very calm at first, then in a blink,

(151)

fell unconscious to the floor. After recovering a few minutes later, he acted as if nothing happened. This could have been the foundation for what was to follow a few days later."

"Doesn't sound like irresistible urge. Sounds like merely fainting."

"I would agree. However, when there are subsequent symptoms, one has to consider the history. In medical situations, where a patient shows up to his primary care physician, and the doctor finds a small lump, it may be just that. A non-malignant lump. However, in time, if not treated, it might turn into something much more malignant. Many diseases and many mental disorders, sometimes give a warning before becoming full-blown."

"Thank you, Doctor. No more questions."

Leland stood up and addressed the court." Defense calls Dr. Shelby for recross."

Dr. Shelby came forward and was advised by the judge, that he was yet under oath. He took hi s seat in the witness box.

"Dr. Shelby, you have heard the testimony of Dr. Lenora Freeman? How did it strike you? Did it seem credible?"

"I was impressed. Of course, I am aware of her outstanding work in the field."

"I must ask, did you find questionable error in her diagnosis?"

"It is hard for me to judge another Doctor's examination without full review of her methodology and summations."

"You have heard that she used hypnotherapy in her sessions with the defendant. How do you evaluate the usefulness or lack thereof of that methodology?"

(152)

"Once again, I would have to know more about the sessions, and under what protocol they were administered. Hypnotherapy can be a useful tool under the correct administration. It usually is a tool, that is considered best used over a longer period of time, than three sessions, so close together. I am not convinced that three quick sessions can be conclusive."

The next question was a pop-up. The good Doctor had given Leland a puffball. It was irresistible urge that drove him to ask. "Taken your answer to the next level, then would six hours be of greater value than three in evaluation of the patient?"

Stoltz was also given an urge, "Your honor prosecution objects to this question. It implies more than the witness has eluded to."

Judge; "I think that train has already left the station. The question was framed properly in response to the witness's own theory. Over-ruled."

"So, Doctor, is the answer yes or no?"

"I cannot deny, that in the case of care to a patient, more time is better than less. In this particular case, the defendant was examined for state of mind. That is a fairly simple task. It did not require more, than the time I allotted to perform that duty."

"No more questions. Defense rests."

Judge; "Folks, the time is late. We will adjourn until nine in the morning. We will hear closing arguments at that time. The jury is admonished, to not discuss the trial proceedings to anyone. Even amongst other jurors. You will get that opportunity in the morning, in closed quarters Court is adjourned."

(153)

Tuesday September 19, 2018, the court was preparing the final stage for the trial for Edward Struthers. The proceedings began at nine in the morning. By that hour, all members involved were seated at their respected places. The judge had entered, and the ritual of standing, then being seated, again was exercised. The jury was lead in from their deliberation room. They took their places in the jury box.

Judge; "Good morning to you all. We are at the point in this trial, to hear closing arguments. Both prosecution and defense, has advised the court, that they would take less than one hour to make their closing statements. So, we begin."

Oscar Stoltz arose from his seat at his table, and approached the panel. He made a presentation to the jury, outlining the facts and circumstantial evidence, that was conclusive of the defendant's culpability, in the homicide of Wade Brendon.

Leland Costello was next to present to the jury. He walked slowly towards the panel of jurists. He bent his right arm and rubbed the back of his head as he approached. "Ladies and gentlemen, this has been a contentious trial between a citizen and the state. It will be up to you to take all information you have been given here yesterday and today. It is my contention, that there has not been sufficient evidence and testimony to place guilt on my client. Please remember, the rule is innocent until proven guilty. That rule, puts the onus squarely on you twelve fine folks. Mr. Struthers entered this room yesterday, an innocent man. Indicted, yes. But innocent, until proven beyond a shadow of a doubt. At no time was he obligate to prove his innocence. Contrarily, it was required that the state prove him absolutely guilty.

(154)

"Now it will be placed in your hands to make a factual decision on guilt or innocence. It is one of the most demanding tasks to be dealt to any citizen. It is a task that asks of you many things. To put aside any prejudices, hearsay, or personal ambiguities. I would put it to you, as being akin to putting together a model. Let us say, that you go to an arts and crafts store and buy a kit. It is a colorful box with a picture of the finished product on the cover. Inside the box is a mumble jumble assortment of many parts. Some small, some larger. You take the kit home and open it up. You pour the assortment of pieces out on a table. You read the instructions. You begin by taking one piece at a time, and placing it together with a connecting piece. Perhaps some gluing is required. After some time of concentration, and trial and error, you have succeeded in putting the model together. You dab on the paint and decals. It is finished. You feel a certain rush of pride. You have used your skills well. But, then you discover a piece of the project lying on the floor. A piece you have completely overlooked. No matter. The model looks just fine. Nobody will know there is a piece missing. Nobody, except you. You will forever be aware that, that one piece is missing. Making your finished project, somehow tarnished, in your own discerning mind." At this point, Leland put both hands down on the rail, separating him from the jury, and in a slightly higher voice, slightly booming voice, "I must tell you, this is what you will be faced with today. You will be given the kit. You will be given instructions by his honor. The kit will be all the testimony you have listened to. It will be the pieces of evidence. Photographs. This model is complicated. So complicated, it requires a team of twelve good people to put it together.

Leland took his hands off the rail. He turned away from the jury and walked a few steps, then turned again towards the panel. "Now, this is the important thing to remember. For God's sake, please be sure, to not leave out any part in the kit. Every piece should be examined with great care. Your finished model must have integrity. All parts accounted for. Any part overlooked will haunt you for years to come. You, and you only, will be aware of the miss-completed model." With those closing remarks, he walked slowly back to his station.

The trial battle was over. Now, it would be the judge giving final instructions to the jury, and then the jury deliberations. The judge instructed the jury, that they were charged to find a unanimous decision as to the guilt or innocence of the defendant. Anything less than unanimity could not be accepted, except to say it is a mistrial. He gave four variant verdict options. "You may find a lesser degree of guilt than the indictment calls for. The defendant is tried for Murder in the second degree. Should you not find, the state has satisfied sufficient proof of the initial charge, you may consider voluntary manslaughter. Your third option would be, that of not guilty of either. Fourth and final option, you may find the defendant culpable of the shooting, but not criminally responsible, due to mental defect. The outcome of that verdict; the defendant would be reprimanded to State Mental Hospital for an indeterminate time period. He would be held there, until the Mental Health Board finds, he is cured of any mental disorders, and is no longer a threat to society or himself. You are under no time constraints. In the event, you do not find resolution by five O'clock, we will adjourn deliberations, and come back tomorrow. In making your deliberations, you are to ignore

(156)

any outside input, that you may have picked up on the news media, or from any conversation from any individual. You are to make your findings solely on the testimonies and evidence delivered in this court. You are admonished, to not give greater weight to any testimony, given by any authority, over opposing testimony due solely, to the fact of authorities' position. You must weigh each testimony based on the merit or lack thereof, you deem to be reasonable, if not factual. A good deal of the testimony, given in this trial by prosecution, dealing with hard evidence, has not been challenged for its veracity. This does not mean, that therefore, you are bound to assume all other testimony, by state witnesses to be of greater credence, based on the factual evidence acceptance. You will need to know when to separate the two. The well-established facts presented, and the opinion based testimony. Outside of the known facts, you must sort through the circumstantial evidence. It is the circumstantial evidence, wherein lies the balance of guilt or innocence. The court charges you to consider all of the circumstantial testimony with a keen eye. Circumstantial evidence is considered allowable, as evidence, that might lead to conviction, as long as it meets the test of reason. One major test is, that there is an abundance of circumstantial evidence, that lead in the same direction. However, it is up to you, the jury, to decide the full merit of all evidence, both factual, and circumstantial. These are certain factors, you must consider and weigh in your deliberations. One note of law. You must not consider motive as a mitigating factor. If you should find the defendant culpable of shooting the victim, you cannot consider the death of defendant's daughter as a justifiable factor. The law is explicit in what constitutes

(157)

justifiable homicide. A person has protection from prosecution, in the event a homicide has been committed in the face of eminent grievous bodily harm to himself or to another. The test is, whether the menacing harm was present, at the time the homicide was committed. That, the homicide was necessary to prevent bodily harm. A homicide committed, when the possibility of bodily harm is not present, or harm has already been inflicted earlier, any ensuing homicide against the perpetrator of the harm, is classified as a revenge killing. This is not allowed under law and is treated as wrongful homicide. You must consider the law as it stands today.

One final note. You must not make any assumption of either guilt nor innocence, based on the defendant not giving testimony. He is not required to give testimony. He is held harmless for standing mute. His standing mute is not to be construed, as anything material to the case. Do not mention it, in your deliberations.

Should you have any questions, pick up the phone in the deliberation room, and a clerk will answer. The court will attempt to answer any questions you may have.

Chapter 23   Jury Deliberations

(Editor's note. All jurors will be presented by number. Their names will be unrecorded here, as a matter of privacy. The numbers given to each juror in the unfolding sequence, do not reflect their sitting order in the panel box. Their gender will be designated as either M for male, or F for female. The jury foreman will be designed by F with gender attached. i.e. FF, or FM)

The jury was lead out of the court room and down the hall to the deliberations room. The room furnishings consist mostly of the large conference table in the middle of the room. With twelve padded, swivel type office chairs. There is a window that looks out over Eighth Street. The room is equipped with an adjoining single bathroom at one end. It would be shared by both men and women. There was a sink cabinet against the interior wall. A large water bottle dispenser next to that. A small refrigerator next to the water dispenser. The icebox was filled with canned sodas, both regular and diet.

The jury foreman addressed his fellow jurors as they all took their seat around the table. "Jurors, I guess it is time to go to work. I think the first order is, to go through the evidence piece by piece, and discuss the relevant weight of each item. I believe we can accept the documents of arrest, and Eugene Police investigation reports as factual. Unless of course, any of you wish to challenge any part of it." No juror showed any sign of contention.

"We should chart out the entire scenario, beginning with the death of Alexis Struthers. This would play to the idea of motive."

M4; "I think we can save a lot of time by discussing the matter as we would any other problem. All the facts and testimony are still fresh in our mind. I know from what

I've heard in there today and yesterday, there is no way I am going to vote for conviction of anything. The victim, cold bloodily murdered the man's daughter. If it had been my daughter, I would have done the same thing."

FM; "You know, the judge warned us about that. The law does not permit revenge killing."

F5, "Yes, that is right. But, how do we punish a man for his retribution against the man who killed his child? I mean what does that say about our conscience?"

M9; "Before we go there, we should consider whether or not the state has proven beyond a doubt, that the defendant actually did the shooting. Remember, all we have is circumstantial evidence against him, other than the fact he once owned the gun used in the killing. The color of the car, witnessed at the scene doesn't carry much water. There are literally thousands of cars that color. Keep in mind, outside of the witness of a sandstone colored car driving down the street, there are no witnesses period. I don't think. I can send a man away on such thin evidence. He may have had good reason for sure, but that doesn't prove anything."

F10; "I think we are side stepping the real core of this case. We have listened to two doctors testifying on the state of mind of the defendant. I liked the words of Doctor Freeman for the defense. She obviously spent real quality time, in examining the defendant. She is determined, that even if the defendant did the shooting, he was completely unaware of his actions. Wouldn't hospitalization be the proper remedy?"

F6; "I agree. However, I do tend to lean towards acquittal of all charges. I have some doubt. There is enough evidence, to point to the defendant as very

(160)

possibly the killer. But, I do not think, there is enough to say without a doubt, he was the man."

FM; "I still think, we should proceed by discussing each piece of testimony and evidence. Well, at least the testimony."

M8; "I understand the analogy of the arts kit. However, I do not think we need to spend a lot of time on each piece of testimony. What we need to determine, is which doctor, do we give the most weight to. There is good reason to believe, Dr. Freeman is somewhat more credible. I say that, due to her spending more time. The hypnotherapy that she used with the defendant, tells me, she dug deeper into the man's mind. I fail to see any reason, not to accept her report and testimony. And in saying that, I would vote for option four, not guilty by reason of mental defect."

F2; "There is another factor. What about the mom. The police seemed to give her a bye. Didn't she have as much motive and access to thee gun as her husband. Who's to say, that she didn't pick up the pistol and jump in the family car, then shoot the victim?"

F7; "I don't think we are allowed to make any assumptions like that. I mean, there was no testimony to base such a theory."

F2; "I'm just saying, that there is a small bit of reasonable doubt. We have to make judgement with no shadow of a doubt."

Eleven thirty, the door was rapped from the outside. The foreman opened the door. It was the security clerk. "It is close to lunch. You have two options. One; you can order off these menus and have lunch delivered her to the deliberation room. Two; You can be escorted to the Hilton Hotel Restaurant. They have a special room reserved, that

(161)

is private. If you choose option 2, you are not allowed to discuss the trail during that time. Should you decide to eat in, you can carry on deliberations. If you opt for the restaurant, I will have a van outside at the front of the courthouse in fifteen minutes."

The foreman turned to the jurors and repeated the options for lunch. A quick consensus was made to go to the restaurant. Probably a sign of cabin fever. Whoever said 'there's no free lunch', most likely never sat on jury duty.

At eleven forty-five, the group was marched out to the van, with the security clerk leading them. It was a short ride, about two blocks, to the Hilton. Inside the hotel, they were led to the private, closed off dining area. They were allowed to order anything, they desired from the menu. The guard would dine with them. His duty was to be with the group as long as they were away from the deliberation room in the courthouse.

Chapter 24   Verdict

Shortly before one, the jurors were once again seated in their respective places around the conference table. They immediately renewed their deliberations. After a few more discussions, the foreman suggested a trial vote to see where they stood. FM; "Each of you take your pads and tear out a clean sheet. Mark on it a column from 1 to 4. Next to one, write murder 2. Number two, voluntary manslaughter. 3. Not guilty of all charges. 4. Not guilty by reason of mental defect. Mark with an x, next to the number you choose.

The jurors took to their pads, and began writing. In a few minutes the notes were all marked and folded, and passed to the foreman at the head of the table. The foreman had pen in hand as he begun to unfold the votes. He wrote on his pad, the tally for each of the charges. After unfolding and reading the last note, he read the results to the crew. "Murder 2 zero. Voluntary manslaughter two. Not guilty of all charges seven. Not guilty by mental defect three. Do you as group feel up to taking a hand count? We may as well know where the votes lie."

The jurors agreed to a hand count. It was taken, and the numbers were the same as the written notes. "Okay. Now we know where we stand. It is up to this group to come to a consensus. We need to convince differing viewpoints as to our own individual reasoning."

Discussions ran on for the next three hours. A few votes were changed. Only two votes did not agree with the acquittal majority. However, it only took another hour of reasoning and the last two votes fell in line. The foreman

(163)

picked up the direct line telephone and reported the verdict had been reached. The clerk immediately came to the door and opened it. "Jurors. You have reached a verdict?"

The foreman replied, yes, they had. They were ready to report to the judge. The clerk led the group back into the courtroom and into their box. The judge and attorneys, having been informed that a verdict had been reached, were back at their respective stations. The defendant had been brought back in by the deputies. The law clerk read out that court was once again in session. The judge addressed the jury. "Ladies and gentlemen, of the jury, have you reached a verdict in the homicide of Wade Brendon, as charged against defendant Edward Struthers?"

The foreman arose and replied, "Yes your honor we have."

"Please hand you r verdict to the clerk."

The clerk walked over to the foreman and received a single sheet of paper. He walked to the front of the bench and handed the paper to the judge. The judge looked over the report. He looked to the jury foreman and asked. Is this your unanimous verdict? The foreman replied, yes, it was the vote of each and every member of the jury.

"Do you find the defendant not guilty as charged for murder in the second degree?"

"Yes."

"Do you find the defendant not guilty of voluntary manslaughter?"

"Yes."

"Do you find the defendant not guilty of homicide due to mental defect?"

"Yes."

(164)

I will now roll call the panel. My question is do you agree to the verdicts as written?" We will start with you Mr. Foreman and go right down the line. Do you agree to the verdict as written?"

"Yes."

"And juror number two?"

"Yes."

"Number three?"

"Yes."

The question was put to the remaining jurors, and each answered affirmative. "The verdict of this court is, that the defendant is found not guilty of all charges. The defendant is free to go. The jury is dismissed. Court is dismissed."

It was a sudden and blunt ending to the affair. Leland was not overly surprised. He knew it would be hard for folks to wipe out of their judgement, the atrocity that had been committed against the Struthers's household. People have one overpowering characteristic, that of compassion. He put in a call to Dr. Freeman's office. He had promised to let her know the outcome right away. She took the call and said she was happy that Mr. Struthers would be free again. Then she handed Leland a slight jolt. "You must have Edward brought to my office as soon as possible. I gave my full report to the court. However, there is one item, I a have not mentioned. I did not think it to be important, and I was never queried about it. There is a danger to Mr. Struthers. It has to do with the identity disorder, I did mention. We did not go into all the intricacies in court. I must warn you here and now, that there is a danger to Edward. I am afraid of the real possibility that he might harm himself. Why so, you may ask."

(165)

"Hell yes, I may."

"It's a bit complicated. The brief version is, that there could be a relapse in his subconscious, that might revive his memory of that fateful morning. If that should happen, he might be faced with trauma so heavy, that he could buckle under. By buckling under, I mean he may attempt to end his own life."

"Damn. We can't let that happen. Listen Doctor, I'll get him to you, even if I have to drag him there. When can you see him?"

"Bring him here at ten in the morning, if you can."

"I'll figure a way."

Chapter 25   Final Verdict

Leland called the Struthers' residence. Myrna answered the phone. "Good afternoon Myrna. Is Edward at home?"

"No Lee. He is out just now. I'm glad you called. I am worried about Ed. He hasn't been himself, since we got home from the trial. He spent a lot of time praying. Giving thanks for his deliverance. When he finished praying, he had a troubled look on his face. Without any explanation, he went out to the car and drove off. I called Reverend Dirksen, thinking he might be going there for counciling. But the reverend has not heard from him. I have no idea, where he could have gone off to."

"I shouldn't worry too much. He might, just wanted to take a drive and clear his head. He will most likely show up soon."

Leland's prophecy was not to materialize. Well late into the night, and there was no sign of Edward. Myrna was beside herself with worry. She could not think about sleeping. She paced throughout the house. When morning rolled aroud, there was still no Edward. She picked up the phone and called Leland. He would be the one to break the sad news to her. Edward had been found. His body had washed ashore on a Florence beach. It had been discovered by a couple hiking on the beach. The Lane County Sheriff's office had been notified. A sheriff deputy from Florence had responded to the site.

"Myrna, I will be at your house in a few minutes. We will thinik it out together."

Edward upon arriving back home, had gone into his den and knelt for prayer. He did not feel any sudden rush of happiness to be back home. His head was in a buzz over the ordeal of the trial. He had to stand this day, before his peers and hear them say, what he always knew. He now, looked to the Lord, to iron out the difficulties whirling in his head. There was something, that did not set completely right. He would seek the answer. It was during this forbearing himself, that memories began to flash back. He was beginning to relive that Saturday morning. He cxould see the gun in his hand. He was driving the family car. He was headed to Karen Morgan's residence.

He had waited for a short time, parked across the street from the house. Wade came out. He could see the gun extended out the driver's window. He could hear the three shots ring out. He could see Wade collapsing to the ground.

Edward felt self betrayed. He had committed a terrible sin. He was engulfed with an aura of putrid, foul, malevolent suffocating stifle. He picked himself up. "Lord, help me."

Edward left the house and got into the Ford, and began to drive. He had to have time to think. He said nothing to Myrna as he left. He found himself on Highway 126 headed West towards Florence. He felt a deep need to be at the Ocean's edge. He had always held the ocean in high respect. He felt it brought people closer to god. After all, it was one of his greatest creations, next to life itself. Wasn't Christ brought to the sea? Did he not walk on the waters? Christ began his crusade for man at the sea. He picked his firt followers from the sea. Were they not men that worked the sea for their livilyhood? Could a man not find ultimate closeness to God in the sea?

Edward parked his car on a lookout point, with a magnificent view of the ocean. It wa high above the shoreline. He sat in the car and took in the wonderous view. Now he must climb down the embankment and walk upon the shore. Once at the water's edge, he cried out "OH my God, what have I done, that I have so offended thee. I have sinned greatly aginst thee. I come here to atone to you. I offer myself body and soul to thy

(168)

judgement. As he said these last words, he began wading through the surf out into, what he prayed would be, the forgiving arms of God. His body would washed back to the shore hours later. He would be found, at the dismay of two young lovers, hiking the sandy shore that next morning. Edward was surely now, facing his final judgement.

Leland drove to Myrna's. This was going to be a tough one. He would rather be back in the military doing KP, than to face the chore at hand. It would be less painfull, to lose a tough trail case, than to have to be, the messenger of such terrible tidings.He approached the front door and rang the bell. She opened the door. She looked bedraggled. It was immediately noticeable that she had not slept all night. He stepped inside and took her by the arm. He wanted a good grip on her before he let the bomb fall. "Myrna. I have terrible news about Edward."

He could feel the tightening of her body. He could feel the tremor beginning to build in her. "Please Lee, no, no, no."

"Myrna, youv'e got to be strong. He is gone now. They found him on the beach over at Florence. It looks as if, he simply walked out into the ocean." With that said, he pulled her around and up close to him. He held her tight without crushing her. He could feel the shivers runing through her. "Can I call someone to come and be with you? I will stay as long as you need me."

The call would be to Reverend Dirksen. He promised he would be there right away.

In such a short span of time, poor Myrna has lost her entire family. First her beloved daughter, and now, her husband. What is left for her to live for? It would be up to her faith, to help her find strength to go forward.

Brad and Matt were in their office when the news of Edwards drowning came across. Matt; "Damn. Brad, what's it all about? The guy is set free, for what looked to be a slam dunk conviction. Then he goes wading in the Pacific Ocean, for what appears to be a case of suicide. What do you make of it?"

"Conscience. A clear case of conscience. I think reality set in. The man was obviously very devout. It may be, like Dr. Freeman explained. Irresisable urge. Blackout. He may have done the shooting while blanko. Maybe things started registering after the trial. Maybe, he began to remember what he had done. It would have been news to him. Bad news for a devout religious man. Maybe, he couldn't live with it. I would lay odds, he went down, praying all the way."

Matt; "How does it all add up for us. Do we close the file on Brendon, or what?"

"We willhave to talk to the DA. My hunch is, this will be an end to the case."

That afternoon the two detectives met with Oliver Stoltz at the DA's office. Oliver had them ushered into his office. "Well boys, I guess you heard the news. Our indicted, but not convicted suspect has apparently sentenced himself. He was scot-free. Why do you think he did it?"

Brad; "I disagree. I think, he didn't feel free at all. His conscience came down hard on him. He couldn't face up to what he had done. It's possible the good doctor was right all along. Maybe, he was blocked out when he did the homicide. Just maybe, it all began to come back to him."

Oliver; "If that damn jury had of done the right thing, he would still be alive. It beats me, that they came out with such a loopy verdict. The evidence we presented was iron clad. It was the worst verdict rendering, I have ever witnessed. We had him dead to rights."

Matt; "Stop for a minute and think about it. I'm sure that every member of that jury asked themselves, what would I do, if someone killed a child of mine. I am sure, in reality, none would

(170)

have taken the same action as the defendant. But they sympathized with him and his loss. I believe the verdict was strictly from the heart, not the head. Human compassion is a strong force to deal with."

Oliver; "That's a good assessment. Most probably right. How do we get people awayh from such wrongful reasoning, when it comes to judging a person for homicide. How do we get them to truly separate their emotional feelings, and deal with the facts. This jury did not act out their duties. They took on the role of judge and jury. The rest of us, may just as well stayed home. I will not take the high road and say that justice is done. In it's own mysterious way. Frankly, I do not believe that is the case here. The actions of the defendant did not deserve a death sentence."

Brad; "Amen to that. Now the question is how do we dispose of the case of Brendon?"

Oliver; "It would be simple to just write it off as a closed file. But by law, I cannot. I have to believe the defendant Struthers, is innocent of the murder. I don't like to believe it. But I must. The jury made that decision for me and the county. So, case unsolved. File open for further investigation. However, I will not expect the department to pursue the question. I suggest, you put the case on the fartherest back burner you can find over there. It would be fruitless to chase shadows at this point. You might put a closure on it, by writing a statement, that incontrovertible evidence, pointed to a now disceased suspect. As far as I am concerned, I think I am going out, and slugging down enough drinks to wash the whole damn thing out of my mind."

(171)

IN MEMORY OF

Gary Obie 2017
He lived life on his own terms. They were good terms.

ACHNOWLEDGEMENTS

I SINCERELY WISH TO ACKNOWLEDGE AND THANK Ron Gorman, of Ron Gorman Design in Eugene, Oregon. Ron is a friend and associate of long standing. We have been friends for decades. We each worked in the advertising business. His was the advertising art section, while mine was in the sales field. We worked many projects together. He is a most accomplished advertising artist. His work is exemplary, whether it is billboard design, magazine, tee shirts, car show brochures, special event banners, or as in this case, book cover art.

Ron is responsible for every book cover, of each of the novels I have published. I amvery happy with the work he has done for me. I only hope, to keep him at it, for as many novels I can write.

I also want to thank Delores Mord. My most avid fan. She reads my material as fast as I can write the pages. She gives me courage to keep at it. She claims, she really loves the material. I am sure, she is mostly being super nice. But don't look a gift horse in the mouth. I will joyfully accept her kind reviews.

Made in the USA
Lexington, KY
16 September 2018